KUTTIEDATHI AND OTHER STORIES

M.T. Vasudevan Nair (b. 1933) is the best known among his generation of storywriters in Malayalam. His publishing career spans a little more than fifty years. Apart from short fiction in which he has excelled (18 volumes), Nair has published novels and novellas (9), travelogues (2), literary criticism (5), books for children (2), and a sizeable number of miscellaneous notes, reviews and memoirs. He is also among Kerala's most popular scriptwriters and directors of mainstream cinema. Nair scripted, produced and directed his *debut* film *Nirmaalyam*, which won the Indian President's Gold Medal in 1973.

Nair's stories have been translated into major languages in India and abroad. He won the *Jnanpith* in 1996. Widely travelled, and deeply read in the classics of literature and cinema, Nair was associated with the editorship of *Mathrubhumi* periodical publications for well over four decades. He has also served as Chair of the Indian Panorama Jury; and on the Boards of Film Finance, and National Film Development Corporations; and the Central Board of Film Censors. Currently, he is the President of Kerala's Thunchan Memorial Trust.

Nair is married. He lives in Kozhikkode.

A seasoned and sensitive translator, V. Abdulla (1921–2003) has known M.T. Vasudevan Nair since his youth. His earlier work has included translations of Malayalam writers like S.K. Pottekkat, Vaikom Mohammad Basheer and Malayatoor Ramakrishnan. He won the Yatra Award (1995) and the Sevarathna Award (1996) for translation. He retired as Divisional Director of Orient Longman in 1981.

The translations in this volume were completed before his death in 2003. He is survived by his wife, two daughters and a son.

Kuttiedathi
and Other Stories

M.T. VASUDEVAN NAIR
Translated from the Malayalam by
V. ABDULLA
with a Foreword by AYYAPPA PANIKER

Orient Longman

KUTTIEDATHI AND OTHER STORIES

ORIENT LONGMAN PRIVATE LIMITED

Registered Office
3-6-752, Himayatnagar , Hyderabad 500 029 (A.P), India
e-mail : hyd2_orlongco@sancharnet.in

Other Offices :
Bangalore, Bhopal, Bhubaneshwar, Chennai, Ernakulam, Guwahati,
Hyderabad, Jaipur, Kolkotta, Lucknow, Mumbai, New Delhi, Patna

© Orieng Longman Private Limited, 2004
Reprinted 2006

ISBN 81 250 2597 9

Typeset by
Scribe Consultants
New Delhi

Printed in India at
Novena Offset Printing Co.,
Chennai 600 005

Published by
Orient Longman Private Limited
160 Anna Salai
Chennai 600 002
email : ollmad@md4.vsnl.net.in

Contents

Foreword

The trend of progressive realism had just blown over when, with the coming of Independence, there was a shift towards greater subjectivity and inwardness in all genres of literature in Malayalam. There was a change of focus from generalised abstractions to felt authenticity in the perception and recording of social reality. A mood of introspection came in the wake of the writings of Karoor Nilakanta Pillai, S.K. Pottekkatt, Vaikom Mohamed Basheer and P.C. Kuttikrishnan (Uroob). The strident voice of Kesava Dev, and Thakazhi Sivasankara Pillai had mellowed, with the former raising the question For Whose Sake? (*Arku Vendi?*) and the latter turning away from beggars, peasants and scavengers to the love story of Pareekutty and Karuthamma in *Chemmeen*. Society was still there, with all its complicated political and economic tangles, but the individual or personal concerns of the members of the upper class or middle class or lower class came to be addressed by the writers. Karoor highlighted compassion and pathos as fundamental elements in the everyday life of his characters, cutting across class divisions. Basheer often poked fun at the behavioural style and vocabulary of the self-styled leaders, drawing attention to the down to earth man and woman. Uroob, in short and long fiction, provided a larger canvas for the private lives of individuals and families, but was sympathetic to the sufferings and struggles of man in society. It was during this interregnum that M.T. Vasudevan Nair and others of his generation entered the scene, particularly of short fiction, to draw the attention of the reading public to the loneliness and alienation felt by individual characters caught in a social transition. Individual human beings with their private agonies emerged replacing the social stereotypes of erstwhile fiction committed to grand ideologies and slogan shouting. The whisper of the soul became audible, which had earlier been swallowed or stifled by public oration and street-side chorus. The new trend immediately caught popular attention, since that came to be symptomatic of the early years of independence. Slogans were replaced by sobs; with a gentle touch of the romantic without excessive sentimentality, the new and young writers wound their way into the sensitive minds of the new generation readers. A remarkably fresh sensitivity was evoked by the new short story, which was soon echoed in longer fiction too. A quiet and un-proclaimed revolution was sweeping through the corridors of Malayalam fiction, which in a way had its impact on the senior writers as well. In a few years the modernist writers with existentialist leanings, questioning current assumptions, came upon the scene: among them may be mentioned Pattathuvila Karunakaran, Kakkanadan and O.V. Vijayan. Vasudevan Nair, however, steered his course away from philosophical obsessions and simplistic formulae about life and society, and has till date maintained his integrity by pursuing his own perceptions and his own style.

The ten stories collected here in English translation by the veteran and seasoned translator V. Abdulla constitute some of the most well-known stories of Vasudevan Nair, fairly representative of his opus. Spread over a broad span of time from 1962 to 2000, they reflect the built-in variety of his fictional concerns and the changing tones of his narration. A true artist careful about the generic nature of short fiction, he attends to the minutest details of his work here more than perhaps in his longer works. Being a novelist and a short story writer at the same time, Nair knows the difference between the two from the aesthetic point of view. What is perhaps passable in the bulk of a long narrative will not be overlooked or forgiven by the reader of short fiction. Here, the reader's focus is sharper than in the longer narrative; every word, every image, the rhythm of the language and the tone of the narrator, count. Nair proves an excellent craftsman in several of his short stories. He has effective control over the incidents described, but more remarkable than that is the close attention he pays to the choice of words, their sensuousness, their scent and their flavour. In stories where the events are not more important than the atmosphere conveyed, the lyrical element is predominant. Grief, resignation, helplessness, loneliness, isolation, nostalgia: these are some of the emotions most powerfully evoked by Vasudevan Nair as a master of short fiction. In the novels, perhaps, some of these may appear repetitious or belaboured, but within the controlled frame of the short story every word does its duty. There is tremendous economy. One word too many can easily spoil the ambience of a short story. Especially when the emotion is delicately evoked, there is no scope for elaboration or admixture of contrary sentiments. The poetics of the lyrical short story does not provide for laxity.

The earliest of the ten stories in this volume is "Kuttiedathi" (1962) and the latest is "Insight" (2000). The other stories in this volume were all written between these two dates. But it is difficult to say that they illustrate a linear development of the author's art or craft, each of them being a finished work at the date of its composition. As they cover nearly forty years of a successful career, it may be argued that together they constitute the high peaks of the author's creativity. Some of them like "Red Earth" are rather short, while some others like "When the Doors of Heaven Open" are fairly long. In the shorter tales the effort is only to evoke a single mood and the tone of narration does not change. Only one moment, one single context, is evoked in all its intensely sensuous power and passion. The central idea is not spelt out in so many words, but interiorised so that the reader has to get at that through indirect means. In "Red Earth" only a minimal space is devoted to the description of the event or its location; the emotional surge is impressionistically hinted at without straining after effect. A rich sense of ambiguity is slowly built up, by mixing fact with fantasy. The goddess of the legend, the ceremony that was disrupted, and the inner desolation of the locale are felt presences in the consciousness of the visiting lady tourist, to whom the whole enterprise takes on the dimensions of an oppressive experience. Within a minimal frame the story achieves its telling effect in a manner characteristic of the author. The same kind of artistry may be found in "Once Again in Search of a Refuge", where too the fleshy details are suppressed and the narration is kept to the bare minimum. The owner of the house, the manager, the neighbours, the maintenance workers etc. are there to provide the framework of the story, but the focus is on the mood of the loner seeking refuge. An unspecified locale, nondescript characters and expressionist sketching of people and objects help to suggest and evoke a certain mood of isolation and alienation without the aid of any incident as such to make the tale rooted. "Kuttiedathi", on the other hand, tells the sad story of an unmarried girl in an old taravad in decline, as told by a young boy, who is an eye-witness to the domestic tragedy leading to the suicide of the girl, but is too young to understand the nature and dimensions of the tragedy itself. The evil fate overhanging the erstwhile feudal Nair household in Malabar is a recurring theme in Nair's oeuvre, and he is an expert in the slow and sensitive delineation of the agonies of characters trapped in this situation. What with her dark complexion and the ugly wart disfiguring her, Kuttiedathi, as she is called by the boy, is earmarked for suffering and sacrifice. Her natural tendency to protest and prevail is offset by the conspiracy of circumstances, as it were. She ends up a victim of the socio-economic tensions of her milieu. A similar preoccupation on the part of the author with the tragedy inherent in the joint family system comes to the fore again in the longest story in this volume, "When the Doors of Heaven Open". The wry humour and irony built into this narrative about the death of the head of the family, which is expected by the relatives, but actually does not come off, since no one knows when the doors of heaven finally open, account for the elaboration of the story. Every relative had turned up, in spite of their heavy and busy schedule, but the patient did not oblige; he recovered to the consternation and relief of everyone assembled and now ready to leave one by one. The old man also understood their eagerness to leave, as nothing expected did happen and there was no need to stay any longer. His words sum up the denouement:

> Master cleared the phlegm in his throat and said softly: 'Are you listening? If I fall seriously ill again, don't send for the children. They've hundreds of things to do. No telegrams, no phone calls. Don't inform them till you're sure it's all over.

There is matter enough here for a novelette, but observing the unities of time, place and action, the author has tightened the structure of the narrative to close in on the focus. Vasudevan Nair knows where to end a story. His endings are generally subdued in tone, without high dramatics, but they make the reader look back once again at the casual beginnings of the narratives. Several of them are not along unexpected lines. Surprises are rare; normally he does not resort to clever tour de force. They story in its totality has its impact on the reader. Some stories may read like episodes in longer works of fiction but with a sense of finality. Some of them dramatise the tension in man-woman relationship. "Bondage", for instance illustrates a favourite theme of the author's, the pull in opposite directions, 'from one prison camp to another', as summed up at the end. "The Deluge" is narrated from the point of view of the suffering wife, who she discovers is cheated by her husband, who in turn goes about with his young secretary. The theme of marital infidelity is nothing new, but the surrealistic ending is especially effective here. In such stories an uncanny understanding of the psychology of women is displayed with delicacy and precision. The interior monologue of the central character is an effective technique in the absence of a hero to play the role of her counter-part. Triangular love relationship is a recurring theme in Vasudevan Nair's fiction, but it is given a subtle treatment in

"Insight", where the old woman gives a bit of advice to young Sudha to take her own bold decision in personal matters. True happiness does not depend on convention, but on one's own predilections. "The Sale" is another story that explores the loneliness syndrome of the business executive's life partner, left to fend for herself, when the boss is away on business trips for days on end. The stream of consciousness technique of narration helps to mix up ever so many disparate elements in the story. "Kadugannawa", subtitled "A travel note", is located mainly in Sri Lanka and is apparently about a journey in search of the past, but ends up without any discovery; all the same it takes on a metaphysical dimension in spite of the dense physical details of the trip to Kadugannawa and the search for the ancestor. Some stories highlight violence and cruelty. "The Enemy" in this selection, with its bizarre account of a visit to a jail, may come within this category. But in all of these stories as a rule the author cares to depict the subtle nuances of human emotions. The metaphors and poetic images strewn all over the narrative linger in the mind of the reader more than perhaps the situations, which invoke them. One may say that the reader's satisfaction is rooted in the artistic workmanship displayed in the small canvas of the short story as in a miniature painting. These features make Vasudevan Nair's short stories some of the best examples of lyrical narratives in Malayalam.

AYYAPPA PANIKER

Kuttiedathi

Valiamma, as I called my aunt, had two daughters, Kutti and Janu. Since they were older than me, I added *edathi*, elder sister, to their names, so they were Kuttiedathi and Januedathi to me. Kuttiedathi's real name was Malu and Valiamma called her that.

Januedathi was pretty and fair-skinned. Her arms, on which the veins showed blue, were as smooth as the tender core of the banana plant. If she came near you, you could smell the fragrance of sandalwood soap. Her *mundu* and blouse were always a sparkling white. But it was Kuttiedathi I liked more.

Kuttiedathi was dark-skinned. In Januedathi's opinion, you only had to touch her body if you wanted to apply collyrium to your eyes! The tips of two big teeth showed outside her mouth even when she was not smiling. If you held her hands, they were so rough, they felt like dry firewood. She always wore a dirty blouse with black dots. You never saw her wearing a mundu that was not stained with mud and soot. She smelt of soot, oil and clothes that were still damp because they had not been spread out properly to dry: odours that made you want to retch.

There's something I forgot: Kuttiedathi had a growth on her left earlobe, a fleshy protuberance as round and big as a pearl. I would gaze at it, fascinated, when she stood near me, or talked, or sat down to do her hair. It was I who always felt disgusted when she fingered it.

All the same, I liked Kuttiedathi.

No one else at home liked her. Valiamma scolded her whenever she caught sight of her. And always for the same reason: she was not disciplined, not modest. Valiamma would add an old saying to her tirade, that destructive weeds would turn any garden into a desert. And as if that was not enough:

'When you were born, even salt and water must have disappeared from the face of the earth!'

Perhaps because she was used to hearing this all the time, Kuttiedathi would laugh loudly. And that would infuriate Valiamma further. She would reach out for the thing nearest her—a kitchen knife or a wooden ladle—and brandish it, saying: 'Get out of my sight! My life was ruined from the moment this creature was conceived!'

Kuttiedathi hardly ever obeyed Valiamma. What she really liked was to play with me. We would sit behind the kitchen playing kothankallu, a game with pebbles, or she would dig into the earth and catch ant-lions for me. All this had to be done without Valiamma seeing us. We had to take care Amma didn't see us either. If Valiamma caught us, it was Kuttiedathi who was scolded, not me.

Valiamma would shout in a thundering voice: 'Malukutty!'

If there was no answer, the next shout would be: 'You wretched girl!'

'What's wrong with you, Amma?' Kuttiedathi would ask, annoyed.

'You're grown up now. Is it any wonder that no one comes to marry you?'

Kuttiedathi could not run around playing with me. It would harm her reputation, no one would come to marry her!

Valiamma would never scold me; she would advise me.

'Vasu, you're a boy, you shouldn't hang around with this girl.' She had a wise saying for me as well. Prosperity would not come to a house where people played games all the time.

Kuttiedathi could never sit quietly in a place. She quarrelled with everyone. Every day she'd return from the bathing tank after having done something mischievous. She'd thrown Anthurath

Meenakshi Amma's silver dish into the water! She'd beaten up Chummu Kutty! She'd splashed water on Mukami Amma, who was scared of water! The list went on like that. No matter how many times Amma and Valiamma told her not to, she'd draw water from the well in the month of Thulam, an inauspicious thing to do!

In the afternoons, Kuttiedathi would wander through the *illam* compound, go to Kali's hut and through Amina Umma's courtyard and then go back home. She could not wander around like that, she was a grown-up girl, of marriageable age! Valiamma told her so, so did Amma. Valiamma thrashed her with a tamarind twig until it broke. But Kuttiedathi would not stop wandering around.

Valiamma usually had a nap in the corridor after lunch. Amma would be in the northern room. Januedathi's room was upstairs. After lunch she would chew betel leaves, redden her lips, sit down on the window seat and sing the ballad, 'Sarojini's Cruel Deed.' She sang it softly. Januedathi could read and write. Whenever she quarrelled with Kuttiedathi, she'd say,

'Kuttiedathi, remember, I'm educated!'

Occasionally I went up to Januedathi's room. Whenever she was not reading her book of ballads, she would sit in front of the mirror, twisting her hair into curls and pressing them down over her forehead. If I touched her by chance, she would shout, 'The rascal has made me dirty!'

I could not touch her bed, or her song book, or the mirror placed on the big wooden box, or her *chandu* bottle or her collyrium container. Actually I went upstairs only to look at Januedathi's collyrium container. It was a lovely thing, with a little mirror the size of a quarter-anna on its lid. But the moment I entered the room, Januedathi would be alarmed. 'You scamp, stop it ... don't touch this, you brat ... you'll upset that now!'

Why couldn't she call me by my name? It wasn't 'scamp' or 'brat'! Kuttiedathi always called me my name. She would call me lovingly, stretching out the name: 'Basu-o!' I loved hearing her call me that.

The moment Kuttiedathi entered the room, Januedathi

would start shouting for Valiamma. Whatever Kuttiedathi touched, Januedathi would scream—according to her, Kuttiedathi ruined anything she touched. Valiamma would say, 'Isn't she younger than you, girl?'

Kuttiedathi had an answer to that: 'Am I not older than her?'

One day Kuttiedathi took a gold-bordered *veshti* off the clothesline and draped it around herself. Januedathi could not bear to look at her.

'You've smeared soot all over it. My God, what will I wear now when I go to Ariyambadath?'

Kuttiedathi held out her palms and asked, 'Where's the soot on my hands?'

Paying no attention, Januedathi screamed louder:

'Amma, she's dirtied my veshti all over!'

'What am I, a low-caste woman?'

'Who knows?'

'Look at this beauty!'

Kuttiedathi took off the veshti, crumpled it and threw it contemptuously at Januedathi's face. I said to myself, 'Well done. She deserves that!'

'What do you lose if I'm a beauty, Kuttiedathi?'

'Don't put on airs with me. I'll hammer your face till you're dead!'

Januedathi quietened down at once. If Kuttiedathi threatened to beat someone, she would.

'Come on, Basu-o.' Kuttiedathi caught hold of my hand and walked off.

We went straight to the mango tree north of the illam compound. Everyone at the illam would be asleep. This was the right time to throw stones at the mangoes.

'Shall we bring down some mangoes?'

'Can you aim stones at them, Kuttiedathi?'

'Why can't I?'

'Can girls throw stones at mangoes?'

'All right, watch out now!'

I was excited. I had thought only boys could throw stones

at mangoes and bring them down. I started to pick up the kind
of stones she would need. She said:

'If we throw stones, we'll make a noise. We'll manage with
sticks.'

If we made a noise, Kunju Namboodiri would come out and
shout at us. He was very mean. He never allowed people to pick
up even the mangoes that had fallen on the ground.

Kuttiedathi broke off some twigs.

'Step aside.'

I moved aside respectfully. Kuttiedathi took aim and threw
the twig at the tree. How high it went! Even Thupran couldn't
have thrown it that high. In those days, Thupran was the one
who could throw the highest among the people I knew.

But no mangoes fell down. Kuttiedathi threw the stick again
and again. The fourth time it caught on a branch. I looked at
Kuttiedathi sadly. What would we do now?

Kuttiedathi was furious.

'Basu-o, climb up that *azhu* tree there. Tell me when that
Namboodiri steps into the yard.'

I went up the short azhu tree obediently and kept watch.
What was Kuttiedathi going to do? She looked around, hitched
up her mundu, tied the ends firmly around her waist and started
to climb the mango tree.

I hadn't expected her to go that far!

I stood on the top of the azhu tree and looked in turns at
the front yard of the illam and the mango tree. Kuttiedathi was
scampering up like a squirrel. Januedathi should see her now, I
thought. All she knew was how to put a *pottu* on her forehead
and read 'Sarojini's Cruel Deed.' She couldn't climb trees or
pluck mangoes.

'Look, Basu-o!'

I saw Kuttiedathi sitting on a branch, swinging her legs and
laughing. I couldn't help clapping my hands gleefully.
Kuttiedathi plucked mangoes and threw them down at a spot
covered by dead leaves, to muffle the sound.

At that moment I heard a laugh on the other side of the

clump of bamboos. I turned and saw Kutty Narayanan.
Kuttiedathi pretended she hadn't see him.

'The girl climbed a tree! The girl climbed a tree!' he shouted.
What was wrong with him?

But he was like that. Kuttiedathi came down the tree,
unruffled. She pulled the ends of her mundu down and gathered
the mangoes. Kutty Narayanan continued to shout:

'The girl climbed a tree! The girl climbed a tree!'

I prayed: 'God, don't let Kunju Namboodiri hear!'
Kuttiedathi wrapped the mangoes in teak leaves, handed them
to me and went straight up to Kutty Narayanan. She didn't say
anything, she just slapped his face.

He deserved it. What if women climbed trees? Evidently he
was wondering how to take revenge. Kuttiedathi must have
realised this. She raised her hand and said:

'Stupid buffalo! Get away!'

Kutty Narayanan took her advice and ran.

However, the matter came up before Valiamma. There were
two changes. One, Kuttiedathi had climbed the mango tree.
Two, she had slapped Kutty Narayanan, a man!

'Malukutty, did you climb a tree?'

'I did.'

'You did, girl?'

'I did. So what?'

Frightened, I went close to Amma, pretending I knew
nothing.

'You're a grown up girl. Do you know that?'

Kuttiedathi was silent.

'There are no elders in this house, but you must at least fear
the pillars that support the roof.'

There was no reply to that either.

'I'll teach you to behave properly.'

Then came the sound of blows. One, two, three.

'Will you climb a tree again?'

One, two, three ...

'Will you fight with boys?'

One, two, three ...

I covered my ears with my hands and stepped into the yard. I couldn't bear it. When I went in after some time, Valiamma was in the courtyard of the *nalukettu*, leaning against a pillar, sobbing and talking to herself.

'Oh Guruvayoorappa! That a creature like this should have been born in this *taravad!*' Valiamma saw me standing there hesitantly and called out to me. I went up to her, full of fear. But she clasped me to her and wept.

'You're a boy, little one ... It's you who'll be the master of the house tomorrow.'

I extricated myself and went to Amma. Amma was wiping her eyes as well. Why had Valiamma wept? Not a day passed without her weeping. Amma explained: Valiamma has no one of her own.

Valiamma had no one. She had no money. My mother had a son. And my father sent her money every month.

It made Amma sad to think of Valiamma. When Amma talked about her, there would be a catch in her voice. One night she told me many things. Valiamma was Thazhevalappu Kuttan Nair's wife. Kuttan Nair was the head of a big joint family. He was a businessman. Valiamma used to stay at Thazhevalappu. When she visited her own house, she travelled in a palanquin.

Amma was a child at the time. She went to stay with Valiamma at Thazhevalappu. The Thazhevalappu folk made a gold necklace with a pendant for Amma. Valiamma stayed on the first floor of the main wing of the house. She never came downstairs. No one ever went against her wishes. The local people liked Valiamma. When she went to the tank for a bath, a person would walk in front of her carrying a large boat-shaped dish containing three measures of oil. The oil would be poured out for anyone who wanted it. On festival days, she would distribute clothes to those who needed it and money to the others.

'How generous she used to be with gifts!' Amma would say.

But Valiamma's prosperous times came to a sudden end. One night, Kuttan Nair came back from work with hiccups. While eating, he threw up. He died at midnight.

Kuttiedathi was three years old then. Januedathi was not yet a year old.

The next morning, Kuttan Nair's nephew took charge of the keys of the house. Even before the body was cremated, Valiamma was sent back to her house with the maidservant, Paru. Amma remembered her coming home with the two children, followed by Paru carrying a bundle of clothes.

'How generous she used to be with gifts, child! It's all her destiny!'

I stole a glance at Valiamma, sitting with her head buried between her knees.

It was then that I thought of Kuttiedathi. She was not anywhere downstairs. When I went upstairs, I heard a sob from the room used for the Bhuvaneshwari puja. It was dark there even in the daytime.

I entered hesitantly.

'Kuttiedathi …'

There was no answer.

'Kuttiedathi …'

I went up to her, put my hand on her shoulder and asked: 'Did Valiamma beat you a lot?'

'H'm…h'm…' she grunted, between sobs.

'Did it hurt very much?'

'H'm…h'm…' She shook her head to say 'no'.

'Then why are you crying, Kuttiedathi?'

Kuttiedathi put her arms around me, laid her cheek on mine and said, 'I won't cry.'

I lay with my head on her breast, wet with sweat and tears, and sobbed as well.

'Does Basu like Kuttiedathi?'

'Yes.'

'No one likes Kuttiedathi.'

Her tears fell on my face.

I often asked myself: did no one like Kuttiedathi? Valiamma scolded her, sometimes hit her. My mother scolded her too. And Januedathi hated her. Maybe it was because Kuttiedathi was dark-skinned. Or because she had that wart on her earlobe.

No one scolded Januedathi. They said a nice young man would come to marry her.

Valiamma liked Januedathi more. Whenever she went to Thirunavaya to have a dip in the holy river on new moon day, it was Januedathi she would take with her. Once, when Valiamma was going to Ariyambadam to see the *koothu* dance in the temple, Kuttiedathi wanted to go with her. Valiamma scolded her: 'Can't you stay quietly in your corner, girl?'

After that Kuttiedathi would never go with her even if she was invited. Valiamma asked her to go along when she went to see Vadekkathi Parvathy Amma's baby son, to visit Cholayil Valiamma when she was ill, to see the festival of lamps at the Ayyappan temple in Kalayakkalam. But Kuttiedathi refused to go. She said: 'Amma doesn't think I'm pretty enough to accompany her.'

If she heard her say that, Valiamma would lose her temper and begin to curse. 'You wretch, not even grass will grow where you stand!'

Kuttiedathi was not afraid of curses. Or even of evil spirits, not even the most troublesome of them, the Brahmarakshas. Being Kuttiedathi's disciple, I was very brave too. She had given me instructions on what to do if I encountered any spririts. If it was a Brahmarakshas, I had to throw a stone at it without turning back to look. For other evil spirits, I had to chant 'Narayana Namah!', Hail, Lord Narayana! Three times loudly. Narayana's name would drive away any evil spirit.

But I was afraid of the goddess Bhagavathi. Bhagavathi lived in the attic. You could not walk by the attic if you had been polluted by the touch of lower castes. You could not take fish that side. You could not lie down in front of the attic door. If you did anything that displeased the Bhagavathi—it was fearsome even to think of—the Mother Goddess would scatter seeds over you. This meant that you would catch small pox!

Only I could enter the attic. Tuesdays and Fridays, it was I who lit the lamp there and burned camphor. Little girls who had not come of age could go in and so could old women. Other women were not allowed to enter.

Once Kuttiedathi opened the door, went into the attic, drained out the oil from the lamp and rubbed it into her hair. Valiamma caught her doing this.

'You've polluted everything. What are you doing, Malutty?'

'Why Amma ... you know there's no oil at home.'

Placing her hands on her head in despair, Valiamma said: 'You'll ruin the place with your waywardness. What's the use of saying anything? The house is falling to pieces, that's all!'

Valiamma had a Namboodiri perform a purification ceremony the same day. In spite of this, she lived in fear the next few days, wondering what calamities would befall them.

Everyone believed that Bhagavathi had hidden away treasure in the attic. Appukutta Panicker would come, cast his cowrie shells and say: 'This house has a *Chovva*, the planet Mars. By Chovva here, I mean the Bhagavathi. She has great powers. She can turn a violent storm into a whiff of mist. There is treasure here. This is a taravad blessed with good fortune.'

One day, Kuttiedathi made preparations to get at this good fortune. She said to me, 'We must dig up the attic.'

I trembled. Imagine digging up the attic, where Bhagavathi dwelt!

'Don't be scared, boy. You keep watch. Let's find out if there's any treasure.'

The thought of the Mother Goddess scattering her seeds drained me of all strength.

'Bhagavathi's ...'

'Why would Bhagavathi need treasure?'

When I thought it over, I felt she was right. It served no purpose for the treasure to lie there, under the floor. While we could do many things with it. But would Bhagavathi let us go unpunished?

'Wouldn't it be a sin?'

'Who's going to take away the treasure, fellow? Treasure indeed! It's just a lie. We have to dig up the ground. And then, when that Panicker comes here again with his bag of cowrie shells, I'll show him ...'

Kuttiedathi's plans were not going to do anyone any good.

She was not even allowed to enter the attic. If women who had periods went in, everything would be polluted. And to dig up the floor of the attic! I could not sleep at night, thinking of it. But I couldn't tell anyone. If I did, Kuttiedathi would be thrashed.

Kuttiedathi decided to dig up the attic floor on the day Amma and Valiamma went to the temple. I had to keep watch. What if Januedathi saw? She would tell Amma. Then, in addition to Bhagavathi's punishment, Amma would punish Kuttiedathi as well.

'Januedathi will sneak on you.'

'I'll thrash her!'

I was convinced a great calamity would befall the house in three days' time. The Friday that was coming was a festival day. Kuttiedathi would be annoyed if I didn't keep watch when she dug up the attic floor. I was afraid of her.

But Kuttiedathi did not dig up the attic floor. The reason was that our uncle, Govinda Ammaman, came that morning. Amma and Valiamma put off their visit to the temple. I was relieved.

Govinda Ammaman was our great-uncle and the head of the joint family. He had moved away to live by himself after the property had been divided. He visited us once a month. It was his ancestral home, after all. Govinda Ammaman was very old and deaf as well. You had to talk to him very loudly. Whenever he came, he would sit in the portico for a long time. If Karuppan was working in the garden, he would call him and ask him to pluck a bunch of ripe areca nuts. He would give him two nuts as a present. Then he would ask:

'Karuppa, do you remember, this taravad once had one hundred and twenty-four members?'

Karuppan would answer in a loud voice: 'Yes, yes. The cattle shed used to be there, in front of the grain house. Your humble servant, Karuppan, was only as old as the young master at that time.' He would point to me as he said that.

Govinda Ammaman never tired of talking about the past. I'd heard so many times: the outhouse used to stand at the spot where banana and drumstick trees grew now. That pit there was made when the old kitchen well was filled up. There used to be a storeroom where Valiamma's hen-coop stands now.

He would step down into the front yard and walk up and down three or four times. Then he would lean over the wall, take a look at the grounds and say, addressing no one in particular.

'It's time the banana tree was transplanted.'

No one paid him any attention. It seemed as if he himself was not concerned that anyone should pay him attention.

'The roof has to be redone.'

If Karuppan was nearby, he would murmur assent.

'Karuppan!'

'Your humble servant is here.'

'Do you know, the master who taught the children lived there, in that room?' He would point to a room on the ground floor. 'All the Nair children in the neighbourhood came here to learn to read and write.'

Amma and Valiamma would have finished making lunch by then. I had often heard Valiamma say:

'The old man comes here only to have a square meal.'

Govinda Ammaman had no money. But he would never talk about it. He would talk of past glories all the time. After lunch, he would lie down on the verandah on a rush mat. Just before he left, he would fling a question into the house:

'Everything all right? Nothing special, is there?'

No one would answer.

'I'm going.'

Often, there would be no one around and he would take leave of the darkness in the house.

Sometimes, as he stepped into the yard, he would call Amma in a soft voice: 'Unnimaya, come here.'

Amma would go up to him.

He would whisper to her, as if he was speaking of some family matter. Amma would go in, return with an eight anna coin and give it to him. He would tuck it into a fold of his mundu at the waist and walk away, making a rat-tat sound with his stick on the ground.

Valiamma would scold Amma: 'Why do you give him money every time he asks? Don't you know it's all wasted in Pangodan's toddy shop?'

'After all, he's the head of the family,' Amma would reply.

The day the attic floor was to be dug up, Govinda Ammaman arrived early. As he climbed noisily up the steps, Amma called out:

'Malutty, bring water in the bell-metal pot.'

Kuttiedathi, who was busy thinking of how best to dig up the attic, cursed as she brought the water. Govinda Ammaman washed his feet, fanned himself with the towel and said, 'How hot it is, even in the morning!'

As usual, Amma asked from behind the door:

'You're coming from home, aren't you?'

'Yes, yes; it's so hot!'

'The children all right?'

'Quite all right.'

Having done her duty, Amma went to the kitchen.

Valiamma cursed. 'The old man has to arrive just as we think of going to the temple!'

Govinda Ammaman paced up and down the yard, came back and sat down. He called out:

'Is Narayani there? Tell her to come here.'

Valiamma came to the door.

'Kuttunnair had come from Perumannur yesterday. To talk about that other matter.'

Valiamma grunted.

'The boy has some land. His father's a Namboodiri. He owns a bit of land with about fifty coconut trees ...' Govinda Ammaman thought for a while, then asked: 'How old is the girl?'

'Malutty's nineteen. Janu will be sixteen in the month of Kanni.'

'Hm ... that's all right. They'll be here the day after tomorrow.'

Valiamma was anxious. She asked her elder brother. 'Won't you be here, *Oppa*?'

'Eh?'

Valiamma asked in a louder voice:

'I was asking, Oppa, won't you be here?'

'I'm busy. But how can I not come when it's so important? I'll be here.'

Valiamma said in an unsteady voice, 'Oppa, it won't go through unless you take an interest.'

'What fate decrees will happen. There's no use making a fuss before things are decided.'

When Govinda Ammaman left that day, Valiamma took a rupee from Amma and gave it to him. And she said to Amma:

'The old man's quite affectionate.'

I asked Amma when she was in a good mood, 'Are we having visitors?'

'Someone's coming to see your Kuttiedathi. A proposal of marriage!'

I searched for Kuttiedathi, found her and said, 'Someone's coming to marry you, Kuttiedathi.'

Kuttiedathi laughed and said, 'Go on, you scamp!'

'No Kuttiedathi, it's the truth. Amma told me.'

The day the visitors were expected, I was happy. Valiamma advised Kuttiedathi in the morning.

'Be quiet and well-behaved. Don't let them see your pranks.'

Kuttiedathi had a bath in the morning. She wore a freshly washed mundu with a coloured border and blouse with red and blue dots. She placed a large red round mark on her forehead with *sindooram*.

I made fun of her. 'Look at Kuttiedathi, what airs she's putting on!'

Januedathi chanted in a singsong voice, as if reading a lesson:

'Will the crow turn into a white crane if it bathes?'

Kuttiedathi did not scold her or slap her. Unusually, it was Valiamma who rebuked Januedathi. 'Get away! What a thing to say!'

Januedathi remarked, as soon as Valiamma went away: 'They can't but like you, Kuttiedathi.'

'Go on, say whatever you like!'

'You just have to take off the wart on your earlobe!'

I was certain Januedathi would get a slap then. But all Kuttiedathi did was look out of the window and say softly, 'Janu, wasn't it God who gave it to me?'

Three others came besides Govinda Ammaman. The reed mat with the picture of a tiger, borrowed from the neighbours, was spread on the floor. Coffee and snacks were served. While they were relaxing after coffee, I peered at them through the wooden bars of the window, taking care not to make noise.

Which one would marry Kuttiedathi?

Only one of them wore a shirt. He's the one, I decided, the one with the shirt.

Govinda Ammaman called out, 'Bring us water to wash our mouths.'

Valiamma seemed to have been waiting for that signal. She filled a small bell-metal pot with water, placed it in Kuttiedathi's hands and said softly, 'Go on.'

Kuttiedathi put the pot down at the edge of the verandah abutting the portico and came back.

They sat there a long time, talking. Then they left. Govinda Ammaman left with them.

He came again after a week. Valiamma ran up to him. 'What did they say?'

'It didn't work out.'

He went on. 'Says he saw the younger one. If it's her, he'll agree ...'

Valiamma was silent for some time.

'What do you say, Narayani?'

'It's not right, is it, to get the younger one married while the older one's still at home?'

'That's true. It's never happened in our family. All the same ...'

Valiamma wiped her eyes with the end of her mundu.

Govinda Ammaman said: 'We can't be so particular. If we can manage one, at least that's over.'

Valiamma thought it over. 'No, Oppa. Someone else will come along if it's in her destiny.'

I realised the one who'd worn a shirt had not liked Kuttiedathi. When I went upstairs, Kuttiedathi was sitting in the dark.

'Kuttiedathi!' I called out hesitantly.

'What is it, Basu-o?'

'Won't he come back?'

'No, he won't. No one will come.'

Govinda Ammaman came again next month with some other people. That day too, Kuttiedathi had a bath, put collyrium in her eyes and a sindooram mark on her forehead. She took out the mundu with the coloured border and the dotted blouse. And went to the verandah with a pot of water.

As soon as they went away, Kuttiedathi went upstairs and began to weep.

A few days later, there was Govinda Ammaman again. And with him were some more people. But Kuttiedathi's mood had changed.

'I'm not going to the verandah.'

'What?'

'No one need come to see me.'

'Malutty!' Valiamma ground her teeth.

'I'll not go, not even if you kill me!'

'Malutty! My little one! I've made an offering to the Goddess.'

'I won't go!'

'This will work out.'

Kuttiedathi's voice rose. 'Will you keep quiet, Amma, and go away?'

Valiamma threatened her: 'You wretch, at this rate you'll turn old and grey, sitting here.'

'Let me turn grey then!'

Valiamma and Amma took turns to coax her. But she would not agree.

Valiamma caught her by her hair and gave her a few blows on her head. Amma intervened. 'Edathi, there are strangers outside.'

Waiting for the water to be brought to the verandah, Govinda Ammaman called out again. Valiamma went up to the door and said in an unsteady voice, 'Malutty's having her periods.'

No sooner did the visitors leave than Valiamma caught hold of Kuttiedathi and began to thrash her. After putting up with it for a while, Kuttiedathi pushed Valiamma's hands away and said, 'Don't touch me!'

'I'll cure your insolence!'

'I'll get myself a length of rope ...'

'Get it over and done with then!'

Valiamma dragged Kuttiedathi along the floor by her hair, then began to thrash her again. Amma intervened once more and caught hold of Valiamma's hands.

'Don't kill the creature, Edathi.'

'I'm going to die!' said Kuttiedathi.

'Let her die!'

Amma freed Kuttiedathi from Valiamma's grip. Kuttiedathi sat down on the western end of the verandah, leaned against the pillar and sobbed. I felt very sad. What a thrashing Kuttiedathi had got!

I went up to her and said, 'Kuttiedathi!'

'Get lost!' Kuttiedathi was angry.

'Kuttiedathi!'

'I told you to go away!'

I could not bear it. I sat down near her and began to weep. Kuttiedathi laid me down on her lap, stroked my back and said, 'Kuttiedathi's going to hang herself!'

Kuttiedathi mustn't die. If she died ...

I said, 'No, you mustn't.'

'I'll hang myself from the beam one day. Only then will they learn ...'

I lay with my head on her lap, silent, full of fear.

'Basu-o, go away!'

I didn't go away. Supposing I went away and Kuttiedathi hanged herself!

Valiamma did not talk to Kuttiedathi for days. Kuttiedathi would wander around the neighbourhood all day. She would come to the kitchen when it was time to eat. Valiamma would serve out something on a plate and say, 'Here, lick it up!'

Amma advised Kuttiedathi: 'You're a grown-up girl. You shouldn't loaf around like this.' Kuttiedathi paid no attention.

Januedathi gave her a nickname: 'The loafing officer.'

One day, there was a heavy downpour. Kuttiedathi didn't go out anywhere. In the afternoon, she called me and said, 'Go and get that mirror.'

While I was bringing her the mirror, Januedathi asked, 'Who's the mirror for, boy?'

'For Kuttiedathi.'

'Tell her to look well at her beauty!'

I scolded Januedathi wordlessly as I walked away with the mirror.

Kuttiedathi looked at her face in the mirror. She combed her hair with a broken comb, wiped her face with the edge of her mundu. She bent sideways, felt the wart on her earlobe and asked, 'Basu-o, will Kuttiedathi look prettier if the wart on her earlobe goes away?'

'Will it go?'

'It will. I'll show you a trick. Go and get the kitchen knife.'

I brought her the knife. She sharpened it against the stone ledge of the drain. She took the spittoon kept in a corner of the room, placed it near the bed and closed the door.

'Don't tell anyone ...'

What was this? I couldn't understand. Kuttiedathi lay down on her side on the bed and said, 'Move the spittoon a little nearer.'

I obeyed.

I watched, dazed, while Kuttiedathi moved the knife towards her ear. I trembled all over and placed my hands over my eyes.

'Am...mm...e!' When I opened my eyes, hearing Kuttiedathi cry out, I saw blood dripping from her ear. I screamed, 'Amme, come quickly!' Even as she pressed her writhing head into the pillow, Kuttiedathi gave me an angry look.

Amma, Valiamma and Januedathi came running. Kuttiedathi lay there, refusing to raise her head. There was blood on the floor, in the spittoon, on the bed, everywhere.

Valiamma kept saying, 'The wretched girl ... the wretch ...'

Amma prayed: 'Guruvayoorappa!' She wet a piece of cloth and pressed it to Kuttiedathi's ear. Valiamma sent Karuppan to Vannan nanu, the local medicine man, to get herbs to heal the wound.

It took nearly seven days for the wound to heal. I saw it when they peeled off the layer of herbal paste they had put on it. The wart had not gone. It hung down by a thin strand of skin. Kuttiedathi looked at it in the mirror only once. The next moment the mirror lay on the floor, shattered. I saw the tears coursing down her cheeks as she stormed noisily out of the room.

Kuttiedathi stopped talking, she hardly spoke even to me. She no longer called me when she went out in the afternoons. If I tried to go with her, she would say, 'Don't come!'

I did not have the courage to disobey her.

One day I had gone to the compound above ours to look for fallen mangoes. It was the middle of the afternoon. When I stepped into the lane, I heard Kuttiedathi's laughter from the serpent shrine. I was surprised to discover Kuttiedathi talking to Appunni.

Appunni was the son of an old woman who lived in a little house near ours. I hated him. I couldn't bear to look at his face. One of his eyes looked like a dead fish that had surfaced on the water. Appunni was a stone mason. He always wore a mundu the colour of red laterite.

Appunni hurried away as I walked up to them. Kuttiedathi asked me angrily: 'Why have you come here?'

'Why have you come, Kuttiedathi?'

'To perform your father's funeral rites!'

I was ready to cry. Hadn't she sworn at me? Kuttiedathi understood.

'Don't cry. I was only teasing you. Don't tell anyone, child.'

'I will! I'll tell everyone what you said about my father!'

'It was *my* father I was talking about. But it's not that. Don't tell them anything else.'

'What else?'

'That ... that I was talking to Appunni. Will you?'

'No.'

I didn't tell. I saw Kuttiedathi talking to Appunni many afternoons, standing behind the serpent shrine. One day Kuttiedathi said Appunni was a good man ... he had bought her glass bangles. She had hidden them in her soap box.

'Will you tell?'

'I won't.'

'I'll get you a rubber ball.'

'Where will you get it?'

'I'll tell someone to bring it.'

'Whom will you ask?'

'There's someone ...' Kuttiedathi put her arms around me and kissed my cheek.

It was dusk. I was seated on the verandah, leaning against the pillar, telling my prayers. Amma was busy in the kitchen. Valiamma was on the verandah cleaning the glass shade of the hurricane lamp. Karuppan came and stood at the gate, scratching his head.

Valiamma asked, 'What is it, Karuppan?'

'I've something to tell you, Mistress.'

'Tell me, Karuppan.'

'You mustn't misunderstand me, Mistress.'

'What is it, Karuppan?'

'This humble servant feels distressed to tell you. I saw something. All the Mistress need do is take heed of what I say.'

'What is it. Karuppan? What?'

'I saw the older young Mistress and that mason Appunni talking to each other. It didn't look proper to me.'

'She's betrayed us!' Valiamma sprang up as if she'd been stung by a scorpion. 'Guruvayoorappa! What calamity will this wretched creature bring upon us!'

Valiamma went in and roared in a voice like thunder: 'Malutty!'

Kuttiedathi appeared.

Suppressing her tears. Valiamma said, 'At least until I'm taken out to be cremated ...' She could not complete the sentence.

'What is it, Amma?'

'You ... haven't you ruined the family's reputation?'

'What are you saying, Amma?'

'What business have you talking to that Appunni?' Kuttiedathi did not say anything. Valiamma gave her two resounding slaps on each cheek. Then screamed:

'Speak. You slut!'

Kuttiedathi did not say anything.

'We'll have to listen to unspeakable things because of you. If you step into the yard from now on, you'll be dead!'

Kuttiedathi rubbed her cheeks and went upstairs not even crying. While Valiamma muttered, 'There may be no men here, but you must respect at least the wooden pillars that hold up our family house.'

After that, Kuttiedathi was not permitted to go out of the house. She lay in one of the rooms upstairs, talking to no one. She would answer no questions. She would not come and play with me.

One evening at dusk, Kuttiedathi was seen at the fence talking to someone. It was Januedathi who saw her. Januedathi said slyly, 'I saw you.'

'What if you saw me?'

'You should be ashamed, talking to low caste people ...'

'Don't try to improve my morals.'

They continued to argue and Januedathi brought up the incident of Kuttiedathi having cut off the wart on her ear. She called Kuttiedathi a black creature. Januedathi was about to be given a slap when Valiamma rushed up.

'What are you doing, you wretch, at this auspicious twilight hour?'

Januedathi wept as she told her: all this was because she had seen Kuttiedathi standing at the fence, talking to a man. Was that her, Janu's fault?

Valiamma placed her hands on her head and sank down on the floor in despair. Amma muttered, 'The family will be disgraced.'

Valiamma suddenly picked up a broom that was lying in a corner and began to hit Kuttiedathi all over her body with it.

'Either change your ways or die!'

I thought she would kill Kuttiedathi and, terrified, I wound my arms tightly around Amma.

'Speak up, you wretch! Will I have to listen to such things again?'

Blows rained on her again.

'Don't hit Kuttiedathi,' I said to my mother, crying.

'She deserves it, the slut!'

Kuttiedathi did not cry. She held on to the door and writhed as the blows rained on her.

More blows.

'Will I hear such things again?'

Another blow.

'I'll die ...'

'Die then, wretch!'

'I'll take my life ...'

'Die, you wretch!'

The broom came apart and the broomsticks scattered. Valiamma screamed, fell on the ground and began to wail loudly.

I had buried my face in Amma's breast. When I looked up, I saw Kuttiedathi still clinging to the door and murmuring, with her eyes closed: 'I'll die ...'

There was neither sound nor movement in the house that night. Kuttiedathi lay on her face on a mat in the corridor.

Valiamma did not eat. Amma called Kuttiedathi to eat, but she said she did not want anything. Januedathi said she too did not want anything in that case. Neither did I. Amma tried to persuade me to eat. I would not. Unexpectedly, Amma gave me a slap on my thigh. I was waiting for a reason—bursting into tears. I ran and fell on Kuttiedathi's mat. Kuttiedathi asked in a tired voice: 'Did you eat, Basu-o?'

'I don't want anything.'

Amma came up and asked me to go to sleep. I said angrily, full of bitterness, 'I'm sleeping here.'

Kuttiedathi held me in a tight embrace.

I heard the front door and the kitchen door being shut. The lights went out. I could not sleep. I felt Kuttiedathi was awake as well. Lying close to her, I could hear her sobbing. Lying in the darkness with my eyes wide open for a long time, I called softly: 'Kuttiedathi!'

'Go to sleep.'

'Did it hurt a lot?'

'No. Go to sleep.'

I snuggled against her breast, wet with tears.

'You must be a good boy, Basu. You must look after Amma and Valiamma.'

I grunted. Kuttiedathi's fingers beat a tattoo on my back.

'Sleep, little one. Sleep ...'

Gradually, my eyes closed.

I woke up with a start as day broke, hearing the sound of wailing. Rubbing my eyes. I sat up and saw Amma and Valiamma weeping, their hands on their heads. Januedathi was crying too, holding Valiamma close. Frightened, I looked around. Kuttiedathi's body swung from the rafter at the end of a rope.

Bondage

From a distance, he had seen the railway gate lying wide open. But by the time he reached it, it had closed. He stopped the car and silently cursed with no one particular in mind. His resentful eyes followed the gateman who, unconcerned, not even looking at his car, was going to close the gate on the opposite side.

He could not even hear the sound of the train. He looked at his watch. It was twenty past six.

He had wanted to start early. It was Saturday, so he had been free in the afternoon. But he had felt like taking a nap after lunch, although he knew it would ruin his evening. He had gone to bed at two thirty the night before and woken up at five thirty. However late he went to bed, he always woke up at five thirty. It had become a habit, a relic of childhood when he had been frightened of even the wooden pillars in the house. When he woke up, he had stood at the window, his eyes misted with distress. He had seen the bright yellow sunlight fade and a light drizzle begin to fall, becoming a downpour in minutes. How quickly nature's emotions changed!

He had toyed with the idea of not going. Spending a Sunday in the city meant having the entire day with Miss D'Souza. As he listened to the sweet, sad melodies of "When the swallows fly back to Capistrano," "Black Moon" and "April Love", the softness and fragrance of her body would make him heady.

But when he remembered that he had let three Saturdays go

by while the darkness of many moonless nights melted into the circles around his pregnant wife's listless eyes, he decided to go.

It was in a spirit of sacrifice that he stepped into the car. He had set out on his journey and had to reach home as fast as possible. He always felt he was in a hurry to get there.

He would be reluctant to start, would cook up excuses for not going from the shadowy corners of his mind and line them up before him. But when he finally decided to go, he would suddenly feel impatient. His wife was waiting for him, his little daughter was waiting. He had to rush, leaving behind the twisting roads and teeming crowds of a city that became noisy at dusk.

Someone called out from the car parked next to him: 'Hello, Sir!'

He turned. It was the tile factory owner he had met when he arrived last year in the city.

'Hello!' He waved and smiled.

He did not hear what the man said because of the roar of the approaching train. He might have asked, 'Are you going home?' He nodded, smiling feebly. It could mean yes or no.

It was a goods train which moved as slowly as boring days and nights succeeding each other. The frightening screech of the wheels over the iron rails seemed to crash into the stone embankments on either side.

The gate opened after an age had gone by. Behind him was a sea of vehicles and pedestrians. If the car didn't start now when he switched on the engine ... he started it with a warning. The little car had obeyed him like a slave the last seven years. But it had showed signs of trouble of late. The engine throbbed into life. It was very noisy. The shock absorbers had worn out.

He had a sudden doubt as he reached the city limits—did he need petrol? He had about seven or eight litres and had to go twenty-seven miles. What if he had difficulty on the return journey? He stopped at the next petrol bunk and put in ten litres. When he put his hand into his pocket to take out his purse, he remembered the medicine. The prescription had been in his wallet for days. Then he had put it away in the drawer of his table. If he wanted it now, he would have to go back four miles, open two doors and the drawer. No.

His wife would probably ask him when he got home, 'Did you bring Baby's medicine?' He would have to tell her some kind of lie. 'It's not available anywhere. Ask the doctor to give you a prescription for another tonic.'

It was easy to make a lie work. His face would shine with honesty when he told one. Nature had endowed him with the mask of a calm face and eyes filled with innocence. When he was a child, his mother used to tell her friends:

'Kesu is the most innocent of my children.'

Bharathi would not wonder why a tonic so commonly prescribed for children was not available in this great city. She believed everyone implicitly. Her life consisted of breathing in beliefs in many things. She believed that it had been a sacrifice on his part to marry her. She thought of him as a great man: in spite of having had every opportunity to marry a woman with beauty, he had made this sacrifice. Perhaps she also believed he loved her more than the coconut grove in its prime situated on thirty-two acres of land on the seashore. May the links of her faith never be broken, he thought.

Two people he knew waved to him from a stationwagon that came up from the opposite side. He had made acquaintances only after he came to this city. He had no friends. This had been the case even in other places where he had worked. He never associated with groups. He did not make much conversation. And so, in the eyes of other people, he was considered an innocent, a good person.

He could see a halo of dignity taking shape around him because of the way he kept aloof. He always appeared very simply dressed in clubs and at parties. He spoke little and with profound calm. All the same, he wove a web of magic with words effortlessly whenever he spoke at felicitations or farewell functions. At parties where expensive foreign liquor flowed freely, he would only drink lime juice, to keep the others company.

But, as soon as he reached his own room, he would take out bottles of cheap liquor from his waste-paper basket. Only his servant knew about them. He detested the boy, who had black, ugly lips, who walked awkwardly, like a mother hen, so that the corns on his feet would not scrape against the ground. He resented him because he had seen the other face of the great man who was so respected in the city's higher circles of society. With his ruddy, bloated face and drooping eyes, he was like a question mark, fearful and loathsome.

There were other question marks like him.

The car moved slowly. Sandy tracts lay on either side. Isolated, scraggy coconut palms flew back as he went along. He had not come far beyond the city limits, but there were no signs of human habitation. He saw an old man lighting the wicks on an oil lamp made of stone in front of a dilapidated temple.

The road was deserted. Occasionally, a bullock cart laden with coconuts came from the opposite side. Only two buses plied on this route.

He drove with his eyes glued to the road.

He suddenly thought of a Muslim colleague he had had in Bangalore. He had started driving at the age of sixteen. Cars were a part of his life. Yet, he was prone to accidents if he was alone in the car. He would think about all sorts of things and not concentrate on driving.

The metalled road ended at that point. The culverts beyond were made of the trunks of coconut palms. There were many potholes; the dispute between the panchayat and the community project officer on who should repair the road had evidently not been settled.

Light from the evening lamps glowed beyond the coconut groves. He could make out the gaps between the trees.

Thatched structures that were shops in front and dwellings for the family behind began to make their appearance. The people and the lights meant the beginning of the village bazaar.

A sudden drizzle came from nowhere. The lights in the shops, the people took on weird shapes through the dim windscreen at the back, spattered with water. The road had been straight after he left the city. It was only when he got to this point that he had to start honking.

He turned left in the middle of the bazaar and had to apply
the brakes at once. A crowd had collected—it could be a
pickpocket, a death, a brawl, a madman, anything. Cursing, he
drew up on the side of the road. What a nuisance! Why did it
have to happen right there? He waited, his fingers pressed over
his eyes.

'You must be on your way home?' An old man. He had
taken off the towel lying on his shoulder, was standing
respectfully holding it in his hand.

He grunted in response.

'I had come to see you last week.'

'I didn't come home last week.'

'I've told them about it. Master, you must settle the matter
between me and the youngster.'

He remembered—it was a boundary dispute between father
and son. The man had come to him on a Sunday evening two
months ago just as he was leaving.

'Can I come and see you tomorrow?'

'Yes, I'll be there.'

'When can I come, Master?'

'Make it in the evening.'

He said it deliberately, knowing he might leave by then.

He looked around to see if the crowd was dispersing and
honked gently. People moved aside. What had drawn the crowd
was something quite unexpected—a large fish.

'Master, is there something I can do for you?'

'No, nothing.'

'I'll see you then, Master.'

He knew it was not he who merited this position of respect.
Many village disputes used to be settled in the courtyard of his
wife's house. Her father had been wealthy and powerful. The
man's achievements were pursuing him now.

Even after seven years, he felt like a stranger when he stood
in front of the sprawling house set by the side of a vast coconut
grove within high walls. The villagers treated him with respect.
He used to feel embarrassed when people hovered in the
courtyard, waiting for their disputes to be settled.

He would remember the image of a naked urchin shivering on a night of pouring rain, his arms wrapped around his shoulders, dreaming of a hearty meal of burnt vegetables and cold rice as he stood near the giant grinding stone on the verandah of the feudal mansion, where servant women were busily grinding herbs.

He had nursed only one aim that burned like a spark of fire within him when he left his grandmother's house, weeping, when he had fought for the small bits of coconut the oracle threw to the children. He walked away, hungry and ashamed that he had not got even one, to the leaky thatched hut into which the rain streamed in: his day would arrive, tomorrow if not today.

And the same aim had stayed with him, making his blood boil, when he had arrived in a strange new town with two pairs of khaki shorts and two blue checked shirts crammed into a gunny bag. He had forty-three rupees left over from the sale of the ancient gold coin he had stolen from his grandmother.

Life had begun then in right earnest. Writing accounts for a warehouse in the daytime, studying at night. That journey to success had astonished many people.

A self-made man.

The good man who helped him through college and allowed him to stay in his outhouse would tell his irresponsible son: 'Learn from him—effort always pays.'

He did not keep the silent compact he had had with the man.

He still remembered the wet eyes of that fair, slender girl.

You could call it cheating or ingratitude.

He had become a stranger to himself.

Goodness had always been an illusion for him.

He reached the spot where he had to turn off to the estate— a small road raised over mud flats in which coconut husks had been buried for softening. The smell of rotting husks always hung in the air. He had to drive carefully. The jeep in which Fernandes had come to see him once had overturned at this spot.

He glimpsed the wall in the distance. At the next turn the headlights would shine on the iron gates.

He honked softly, to alert Achuthan who would be in the watchman's shed. By the time he reached the gates, one of them had swung open. It was not Achuthan today, it was his talkative younger brother.

A cool breeze blew through the coconut grove. The air was always humid here, since they were next to the sea.

It was after he had got to know Miss Margaret D'Souza that the moist sea breeze had come to his aid.

He had stood before his wife one day with a tired face.

'What's the matter, aren't you well?'

'A breathlessness. I had asthma at night. Nothing serious.'

He seemed to be breathing with effort.

'It's a few days since this started?'

'Two or three.'

'Why didn't you consult a doctor?'

'No, I don't need to. I tell you, it's nothing.'

'You're always like this, you never look after yourself. You have to see a doctor tomorrow.'

She was full of complaints ... He would never attend to his own needs. She was sure he was working too hard. She was convinced he was travelling too much on the days he did not come home at night. He was probably not eating regularly during the day.

He finally agreed he would see the doctor the next day.

The next day: 'Did you see the doctor?'

'Yes. It's nothing serious. Just asthma.'

'Nothing indeed! Didn't he give you any medicine?'

'I'm taking some tablets.'

She believed the tablets he took at night were for asthma. The words printed on the bottle indicated that the tablets would prolong his pleasure at night. Her education in English had not gone beyond the tenth standard.

He would never get rid of the asthma as long as he inhaled the sea air while he slept. The doctor said he had to live in the city. How would that be possible?

'To hell with the asthma!'

'You mustn't say that. What is life without health?' she said agitatedly.

They could rent a house in the city and live there. But who would look after things here then? Almost twenty people worked here every day. If she left it all to the manager, she would be the loser.

'Your property'

'Ours!'

Mine.

That was true. Finally, she found a way out. He would have to move out until he was better. But he must come home often. He must not fail to do so. Her eyes were brimming with tears.

He thought it an achievement that his face did not betray his happiness.

Let me see that chap who wrote that woman was a problem to which there was no solution and rubbish like that, he thought!

He pretended to accept her suggestion with distress, to agree only because he did not want to disregard her pleas.

The roar of the sea came nearer. Being the monsoon season, the sea was rough. As the car climbed, the headlamps threw a beam of light on the small garden behind the wire fence. At this point, the headlights would always pick up Caesar's eyes and make them glow like emeralds, from where he lay on the verandah. It was a sight that never failed to give him pleasure.

The garage doors were open. By the time he took the car in, the servant Gopalan came running up with a hurricane lamp. He saw the man peering at the back seat. There were no parcels to be taken in.

It was still drizzling.

Caesar's loud barks reverberated in the wet air.

He called out, 'Caesar!' and the dog suddenly fell silent.

Insects fluttered around the petromax lamp hung in the verandah. As he climbed the steps, Caesar wagged his tail, growled and tried to break free of his chain. He went up to the dog and stroked him. He would usually open the packet of biscuits he had brought for Baby and give him one. But of late he had been coming empty-handed and the dog seemed to have realised it. Looking into his eyes, he thought he saw cruelty in them. All right, he seemed to say indifferently, let things go on as they are! Caesar had grown up lying on his lap and drinking milk from a feeding bottle. He was three months older than Baby.

He saw Bharathi come up to the door, look at him and go back. He looked at Caesar's face again. Nostrils distended, he was sniffing the air.

When he went up to him to stroke his neck once more, the dog gave an unpleasant growl, put out his tongue and breathed heavily. He took note of the long, large, curved teeth, the leashed strength of the huge body and quailed before the mistrust in his eyes.

Underneath the petromax lamp, the floor was littered with dead moths, singed wings and wriggling bodies.

He walked towards the door, calling: 'Baby, my little one!'

Bharathi came to the door and said, 'She's eating.'

He looked at his watch. It was ten past seven.

'So early?'

'It's not that early. Do you want coffee or shall I make Horlicks?'

'A glass of drinking water will do.' He put on as pleasant an expression as possible. Bharathi went into the kitchen, dragging her huge belly. She seemed to have grown weaker than when he last saw her. Her eyes were sunk deeper in their sockets. Her skin looked rough, as if it needed to be oiled.

He took off his shoes, put them under the bed and called out, 'Baby, little one, are you eating?'

He went through the corridor into the dining room, took the glass Bharathi brought and drank a mouthful. Baby had finished her meal. Naniyamma was helping her wash her hands. He had another mouthful of water and set the glass down on the table that was covered with a black plastic sheet. Baby came up to him, her large, dark eyes gleaming and a faint smile on her lips.

He remembered that he had not brought her medicine. He

caught the child's hand and went into the bedroom. Once he was sure Bharathi would not overhear, he asked: 'Do you have a stomach-ache these days?'

'No. Amma gives me medicine.'

'What medicine?'

'That one.' She pointed to the bottle of Ayurvedic medicine on the shelf.

He sat down on the cane chair holding Baby close to him and thought about all sorts of things. How he had never forgotten to fulfil Miss D'Souza's slightest wish. How memory had never played tricks on him when he tried to get hold of the things she said she liked.

He stroked his daughter's hair, his eyes closed. He had nothing to ask her nor did she have anything to tell him.

'Aren't you going to school?'

'Yes, I am.'

'Does the Master scold you?'

'It's not Master, it's Teacher.' She had told him that many times.

'Do you know all the poems in your book by heart?'

'While we were playing, Teacher taught us the bird's song.'

'What lesson are you learning now?'

'The Fishing Boat and the Precious Stone.'

'What?'

She repeated the title. He sensed Bharathi behind him. She had not asked about the medicine. Or why he had not come the last three weeks.

God! Had she begun to understand how things were?

Her silent look of helpessness disturbed him.

'Do you feel better now?'

He answered like a fool, 'Eh? What? It's not bad.'

'Do you have asthma at night?'

'It's not too bad.'

He spoke without looking up. A cool breeze was blowing through the window opposite. When it was open, the sea was visible. Beyond the barbed wire fence, the waves broke over the sand.

'Shall I close the window?'

'No.'

'Move over to the other chair. If you sit there in the breeze, you will catch a cold.'

He wanted to laugh and cry at the same time. He had often wished she would be a jealous wife, full of accusations and barbed words. He felt helpless before the hurt and faith in the sunken eyes this woman had.

He waited for her to ask why he had not come for the past three weeks.

'The General Manager came last Sunday.'

She did not ask, what about the Sunday before that one.

'I was afraid you were not well. I even thought of sending Gopalan to find out.'

'I wanted to make a quick visit but the car was in the workshop.'

'A man came for the coconuts even last week. I told him we'd sell only after you came.'

'Couldn't you have sold them?' he asked, grabbing at the chance he had been given. 'There's no point letting them go dry. And I don't have a minute to spare since it's the end of the financial year. We'll never get through everything in time unless we make the staff work even on Sundays.'

It was the distance of twenty-seven miles that protected the imaginary picture he always drew of his busy life in the city, with its pressure of work, its burdens, its responsibilities and the constant fear that he would fall ill.

'Don't you want a *mundu*?'

'Yes.'

Baby freed herself from his grasp and went in.

'Where are you going, little one?'

'I haven't given Caesar his food.'

Caesar and Baby were companions. The animal, which had the strength of an ox, never obeyed anyone's orders, but would listen to anything Baby commanded him to do. If he didn't allow Gopalan to chain him in the mornings, Baby just had to call out to him.

He changed into a mundu, wrapped a freshly laundered towel around himself and went to the portico. Baby was seated on her haunches, tickling Caesar's neck. The dog got up when he heard his master's footsteps.

'Caesar!'

The dog looked at him, then stretched its head out to Baby again. He said to himself that Caesar would be the first in this family to understand what he was like.

'Don't you give Caesar a bath these days, Baby?'

'Yes, on sunny days.'

It must have been the close association with Caesar that was making Baby more and more reserved. He felt that her mind was much more mature than that of a five-year-old.

He called out to Caesar again, but he did not move. He pulled the dog up by its collar. It opened its mouth wide, baring its cruel-looking pointed white teeth. He looked at the animal with an air of casual authority.

I'll teach you one of these days!

The mother called out to Baby from the kitchen.

He walked up and down near the portico steps.

'Father, your hot water is ready.'

He felt refreshed after he had a bath in lukewarm water.

His wife came in to say that dinner was ready. He was combing his hair. Whenever he looked into the mirror, he would secretly rejoice at his good fortune in having such a youthful-looking face.

Bharathi picked up Baby's mattress, which was folded and placed on one end of the bed, and spread it on the floor. When she bent down, she looked as if the weight of her huge stomach might topple her over. Her bones stood out on her emaciated body.

'Won't the maid come? You shouldn't be ...'

Bharathi did not reply. She was in her eighth month of pregnancy.

There were only vegetables for dinner. She put down a bowl of scrambled eggs on the table and said, 'There's no fish because of the rain.'

She turned the lamp around so that its shadow would not fall on the plates and came and stood next to him.

'You're looking run down.' She always said that life in the city had ruined his health.

He did not ask about her health. He had arranged for a woman doctor who lived five miles away to come and examine her once a week. There was a midwife living nearby as well.

'Did the doctor come?'

'She came this morning.'

'Write and ask your aunt to come.'

'I've already written.'

'I'll take leave from next month,' he said to comfort her.

He feigned an air of enthusiasm. 'The white man who's my new boss is an unpleasant fellow. If he doesn't grant me leave when I ask for it, I'm going to tick him off and walk out.'

He had already drawn for her a frightening picture of the Britisher who was his manager. He was always persecuting his assistant manager. He would never grant him leave or allow him to go out of town even on holidays. If he gave in even a little, the man would take advantage of it.

'Don't pick quarrels with him. We don't want trouble, that's all.'

'How will you manage things here without anyone?' Whose voice was that?

'The midwife comes every day. And Aunt Ammu is coming next week anyway. I can always send Gopalan if I need anything urgently.'

'H...m...m.'

'Just come here now and then, that will be a great comfort.'

He started to roll a big ball of rice for Caesar and she said, 'Finish that rice. I'll serve some more for the dog.'

'No.'

'Do you want some more mango pickle?'

'It's very good. No, I don't want more.'

He threw the ball of rice into Caesar's aluminium plate and went to wash his hands. When he came back, Bharathi had sat down in his place. Naniyamma was serving her rice on the banana leaf he had used.

Baby was in the inner room, looking at the pictures in an old English magazine.

'Isn't it time for you to go to sleep, little one?'

She closed the magazine, went up to her mattress and stood there uncertainly. 'Go to bed when you are ready,' he said.

He walked around the room, uncertain what to do or say. Maybe it was better to leave the child alone. He went up and drew a chair into the portico. In the faint light filtering through the coconut palms, he could see the waves, intertwined with each other like mating snakes, beating on the shore beyond the fence.

A long gleam of light from the revolving lamp in the lighthouse two miles away stretched out over the black expanse of the sea from time to time. They said it guided ships on the high seas.

On nights when he had sat here, listening to the roar of the sea and watching the waves rise and crash down on the shore, he had always felt he was in some unknown corner of the world.

Miss D'Souza would be seated in her well-appointed room now, reading. Or she would be immersed in the pathos of some sad song.

Miss D'Souza had written to him about her solitary nights. Her name, Miss D'Souza, would be typed in red at the top.

I always experience your presence in this room. When I open the drawer, your letters are there, your presents are in the almirah; even the records I listen to at night were ordered by you. The string of pearls around my neck, my best satin jacket: all these remind me of you.

When I lie down at night in the bedroom, I can see the marks your feet made on the wall in the glow of the lamp. Do you remember how I too placed my feet against the wall one night to make marks? I always see you in this room and in my heart.

My dearest darling, when will the doors of your house open for me?

Margaret D'Souza, this is my house. Those who will receive

you at the door will be my pregnant wife and my five-year-old daughter.

The husband who was going to marry her was the head of a family twenty-seven miles away—when the Goan girl learned this … he dared not think of it. He had never thought of it.

He shivered. He could see his fingers trembling as he held the window bars.

He must tear off this mask one day and tell Miss D'Souza the truth. He would then stand before Bharathi and declare: I am not the good person you think I am. I have never loved you.

From that moment, he could live as a free, simple man.

He prayed he would find the strength that day to describe the nights he had spent in a drunken stupor, the furtive moments when he had knocked at doors behind which pleasure was sold.

Bharathi came from the kitchen after her chores. In her hand was a glass filled to the brim with milk.

'Is Baby asleep?' he asked.

'Yes. Isn't it time for you to go to bed?'

Time moved so slowly here. By the time night started in the city, this village would be asleep.

Bharathi spread a white sheet on the bed, took down a pillow from a heap stacked on the almirah and placed it at the foot. Then she spread a large, thin mattress on the floor, near Baby's.

She went in again to give Gopalan and Naniyamma instructions. Milk the cow early. Keep the water boiling. Gopalan, go to the butcher in the morning and ask him to send meat and liver quickly.

Her keys jangled as she locked the storeroom. She lowered the wick of the small lamp in the anteroom.

'Why don't you lie down?'

He obeyed silently. A cool breeze wafted in through the window. The sea sounded now like the roar of a crowd in the distance.

She called out before she closed the front door: 'Gopalan, let Caesar off the leash.'

Caesar growled on hearing his name. He knew the vast kingdom of the coconut grove would now be his. As soon as he was unchained, he barked loud enough to frighten even the shadows.

'Shall I turn off the lamp?'

He grunted.

She stroked Baby and straightened her limbs. Then she turned down the lamp and lay down, murmuring, 'Guruvayoorappa, protect us.'

The light from the small table lamp in the anteroom shed its glow over this room.

Baby always slept on her side, curled up, and would not cover herself even when it was cold.

His wife and child were asleep an arm's length from him. The newest addition to the family moved inside his wife's swollen belly. He found it difficult to reconcile himself to these facts.

Nor could he quite accept the image of the lover who parked his car at a distance, walked like a shadow, hugging the edge of the road and knocked at Miss D'Souza's door.

All he could imagine was a scrap of palm leaf floating over many-coloured bubbles of water.

God!

He turned on his side. Bharathi would not be asleep. He longed to plunge into the depths of her silence.

Her thin figure had always evoked his sympathy. He felt her huge belly growing and enveloping her completely as he watched. She was not ugly. But he had never found the slightest element of beauty in her. She had not become a part of his life, not even at this moment, when she was carrying the difficult burden of a second child. Her presence had become painful to him. All he could feel for her was pity.

But when he thought of Miss D'Souza lying on her thick spring mattress, gazing at her footprints on the white wall

If Bharathi evoked pain, Miss D'Souza brought only delight ...

There was something intoxicating about every part of

Margaret's body. Even hours after he had said goodbye and left
her, her fragrance would linger in him. A kiss from her moist
lips could gift everything a woman could possibly bestow on a
man.

The rhythmic breathing of the mother and daughter filled
the room. The roar of the sea beyond the closed window was
like the beat of a great heart. The fragrance of Miss D'Souza's
clothes, of her waving hair, wafted out of the empty air and crept
towards him. He would write to Margaret as soon as he returned
to the city. Forgive me, forgive me ... Margaret would shudder
when she learnt the truth behind the deception. There would be
dark circles under the eyes of the unmarried woman past her
prime, standing on the wet sands of the seashore.

Bharathi would forgive him. He had to write Margaret a
detailed letter and come to the village on a month's leave. He
would live here like a husband and father. By the time he went
back, Margaret's anger or sorrow would have subsided. Perhaps
he would not run into her after that. She would not find it
difficult to get herself another companion.

Another companion beside her, listening to "Dreams that do
not lie" and "Black Moon" ... he could not bear to think of that
either. He tossed and turned, full of resentment.

The doors of his house would never be opened to receive
her. She did not know that he had no home.

And yet he could not even think of her giving another man
pleasure.

Worlds of light and darkness danced before him as he closed
his eyes. He woke up at five thirty in the morning and lay with
his eyes closed for another half hour. Bharathi must have woken
up at five. He got up when she brought him hot coffee. He
usually lay in bed until seven on Sundays even if he did not
sleep.

Baby was asleep. He got up, picked up his shaving set and
soapbox. By the time he shaved, Naniyamma had got hot water
ready for him. He had a bath and changed into the freshly-
washed clothes Bharathi had laid out for him.

His breakfast had been prepared very early in the morning.

It was just six thirty. He sat down at the round table to eat and Bharathi came to the door. He thought her face looked very unattractive beneath the dishevelled hair.

The thoughts he had had at night must have been distant, meaningless dreams.

'Why did you get up so early?'

'I have to go.'

She was silent.

'I'll come this evening.' (Would he?)

Baby was up by the time he was ready to leave.

He picked her up, stood her on the table and said: 'Daddy's going. I'll be back this evening.'

Baby rubbed her eyes and clung to his shoulder.

'What shall I bring you, little one?'

'M…mm…m…' She did not really say what she wanted.

Perhaps the veils of secrecy with which he thought he had hidden his life had already slipped down before his wife, his daughter and Caesar, who had grown up on his lap. He was not prepared to accept defeat. He said firmly:

'Bharathi, I'll come in the evening. Is there anything I should tell the doctor on my way?'

'No.'

'Anyway, I'll see her. I'd forgotten there's a case coming up tomorrow. I have to see the advocate.'

He went down the steps. Caesar growled as he walked to the garage—he had forgotten to give the dog the usual share of his breakfast. He saw some emotion he could not identify in Caesar's eyes and turned and looked at the dog resentfully.

Gopalan opened the garage door and shouted to Achuthan to open the gate.

The air was thick with mist and drops of moisture. A cold wind whistled past his ears. The car flew over the sandy, deserted road. The machine, reading his mind, seemed to long to reach the city. He was not even aware of having passed the doctor's house.

As the wheels sped over the wet road, the home he had left behind faded in his memory. He glanced at the back of the car casually and saw the jar of *kadumanga* pickle, neatly wrapped. What a nuisance!

This road, filled with tired bullocks pulling carts laden with coconuts, dark-skinned women carrying loads of beaten husks on their heads, villagers with dirty towels covering their head and necks, led to the city ... He speeded up. The pitiful cries of a stray dog that had cut across the road faded in an instant. He could go as fast as he liked on this road, that lay soaked in the tears of the night. Towards gatherings of the rich on hotel lawns as soft as spring mattresses; towards company offices where he would be greeted with respectfully bowed heads and extended hands; towards home, where liquor bottles were hidden in the garbage bin and glasses reeking of drink in the bathroom; towards dark alleys with open gutters where pimps lurked, waiting to sell the pleasure of a moment.

Towards a mattress heady with the scent of French perfume, lying under a wall where footprints echoed the memory of a time when swallows flew back to Capistrano ...

From one prison camp to another.

The Enemy

As the bloodstained knife rose from the depths of his ribs like a tongue of fire to plunge in again, he pleaded: 'Don't kill me, Suleiman, don't kill me!'

'Die, you beggar, die!'

He stood waiting at the door until the last spasm of the writhing body stilled.

The picture of a murderer!

He wakes with a start in the middle of the night as the watchman taps on the walls to show him how attentive he is to his work. When he closes his eyes again to escape into the valleys of sleep, the bloodstained knife gleams in the darkness. The picture of a murderer. Another face beneath the white sheet on the mortuary table, over which spreads a red wetness. The face of death, with teeth bared and half-open eyes.

The car was going slowly. He sat silently in the front seat, saying softly over and over again in his mind, Suleiman, I can imagine you standing guard at the door with your knife raised, waiting for the final spasms to cease. I am coming now to see your face as it waits for death.

In front of him, the rays of the afternoon sun danced over the melting tar like colourless shadows.

Behind him, Krishnankutty and Vasu kept talking. They asked him something every now and then in an effort to make him join in the conversation. Since he replied in monosyllables and grunts, they finally left him alone.

They were talking about the tough people who lived and died by the strength of their arms, the sharpness of their knives.

Death had never hurt him. The reason being, he had never loved life. He had stood under the casuarina trees one day imagining his mangled body washed up on the shore by the waves. He was then the sixth member living in a lodge for which five people shared the rent.

He had got up and walked out from the bench in the front verandah. In his stomach lay the smouldering ashes of a hunger that had burned a whole night and two days.

They had been days of hunger. Days when, short of money, he had walked sixteen miles to see an acquaintance who had not been there and trudged back in a half-conscious state. Later, they had become memories, amusing stories to relate at dinners.

He had not thought that a meeting which had taken place years ago would forge new relationships in his life.

He had gone into the room very reluctantly with an acquaintance.

The man was seated with his stockinged feet stretched out on the table. The fan whirred overhead. An expensive cigarette glowed between his fingers. He had said to himself contemptuously, 'Another money-bag!'

'Sit down.'

Introductions. 'Don't you know Abdul Razack, who writes for the magazines?'

The laughing eyes had wandered over his dry mop of hair, his shabby clothes, the stubble on his withered face.

He had felt uneasy.

'You're a philosopher? Will your thoughts satisfy your hunger?'

Those were the days when he used to spend time conversing the public libraries. And here was this money-bag now! Hiding his resentment, he listened with indifference. When he got up to go, the man stopped him.

'Wait, I'm coming out too.'

Hours later, as he got out of the car at the gate of the lodge, the man had called out, 'Hey, Razack!'

Surprisingly, he had not resented the intimacy, the familiarity in that voice.

'Can't you work?'

'What sort of work?'

'Any sort. Nothing to pick and choose.'

'But I must first get a job …'

'If you do, will you set your philosophical thoughts aside and work five hours a day, six days a week?'

He laughed foolishly.

A night when he did not feel the pangs of hunger. Inside, the card players were making a noise. It was years since he had lain flat on his back on the bench looking up at the sky. The same sky he had watched through the leaves of the casuarinas in the orphanage looked beautiful now. He saw stars blossoming in the expanse of blue.

At the back, Vasu was telling stories. Kunhamu was the chief of the toughs. There was no one who could confront him. Suleiman challenged him. They fought all the way from the Kallayi bridge to Mooriyad. Kunhamu took out three knives, but Suleiman knocked them all out of his hand. It was from that day that Suleiman became Suleiman Moopan, the leader.

The last meeting.

When Sahib drove through the crowded streets at frightening speed, he cautioned him: 'Slow down a bit.'

'Afraid? Didn't you once try to commit suicide?'

'You destroyed me. You made me work. You persuaded me to get married. Now life has made me its prisoner.'

When we reached the gate of the hotel, he was insistent: 'Come on.'

'I have to get home soon. My younger son has fever.' He opened the door hurriedly, got out and asked, with his hand still on the door handle:

'Lend me a hundred rupees.'

'Get lost!'

'I need it badly.'

'What about the two hundred you've already taken?'

'It's still there.'

'What do you do with your four hundred rupee salary?'

'Don't talk of this and that. Give me the money. I'll return it on the first.'

'Sure?'

'Sure.'

'All right, I'll write off the past. But I'll kill you if you don't give this to me exactly on the first.'

Sahib called out as he was going, 'Look, Razack, we're cleaning out the bathing tank tomorrow. Come for lunch.'

He thought about himself as he hurried to get home before eight. Those nights when he had wandered around in the light from the pale street lamps while the deserted city was fast asleep seemed so long ago!

The house on the edge of the gravel path where you turned left at the road. He always had a sense of wonder when he went in through the gate. My house, he thought! My family. He thought of the long line of children moving through the verandah of the orphanage into the kitchen, holding enamel plates in their hands. The nine-year-old with festering sores on his knees and cheeks would always be the last, pushed to the back in the crowd. At the age of sixteen, he had stepped into the street with a certificate bound in khaki cloth.

At the back, Vasu was relating another story.

Even the police were afraid of him. With his arm around the girl, he warded off their blows. There were six of them.

'Sir, you didn't hear about the incident?'

'H'm...m.' He grunted assent without turning around.

In the end they hit him from the back with an iron rod and he fell down. But they didn't let the girl go. The fellow had to take off the towel wound around his head and stand respectfully before the chief.

He was lying on the easy chair in the verandah and looking at his son doing his second standard lessons. His wife was inside, listening to the radio with the younger one, who had fever, lying on her lap, covered with a flannel shawl. She was singing softly, trying to echo the radio singer. Her long, slender fingers moved over the yellow shawl in time with the music.

The messenger of death had arrived gasping at that moment, borne on the wings of darkness.

The funeral procession moved behind the bier over the broad path dividing the fields. He stood at the edge of the compound staring at the water tank that was to have been emptied that day, at the fishes that had escaped death darting through the water. When the courtyard and the compound were finally emptied of people, he walked back through a coppery twilight.

The moonlight laughed from the window like a shameless whore. He felt as if he was lying on the mortuary table under a white sheet.

You stood guard at the door, Suleiman, with a bloodstained knife in your hand, looking at my writhing body. Throughout the night, to make sure I didn't escape death.

As the road approached the seashore, he felt cool, relieved. The remains of a dog that had been crushed to death under the wheels of a truck the previous day lay scattered over the road. Beyond the coconut grove, vultures satiated with dead flesh sat pecking at foul-smelling heaps. He held his breath to shut out the smell and looked at the gleaming sea.

The milestone marked another fourteen miles.

He could breathe now, the foul-smelling zone was over.

At the back, his companions were talking about jails. Krishnankutty, who had once been a political worker, had been in jail for a month in 1942.

Vasu said: 'I've never seen a jail. This is my first experience.'

He thought it was his first experience as well.

In order to ward off nightmares, he drew pictures of the enemy twisting and turning in agony over and over again in his mind.

He had never seen a courtroom. He went to the court one day, to see the enemy standing in the dock.

Many people were seated on the four or five benches meant for visitors.

It was not the courtroom of his imagination. The Judge sat writing in an enclosure behind brass railings. Behind his head, he could see the motto: *fiat justitia ruat coelum*, let justice be done even if the heavens fall.

He stood just beyond the door, behind the visitors.

The first person he noticed was the young man in the witness box.

The advocate was questioning him in a low voice. The witness answered softly as well. He could make out what they were saying only if he listened attentively. He thought of a courtroom scene in some movie, where everyone shouted.

That was when he saw the prisoner's dock. He was surprised—even though it was right in front of him, he had not noticed it earlier.

He first saw the prisoner from the back. Hefty arms. Huge fists, knotted with thick veins.

One of the visitors seated on the bench smiled at him in recognition. He moved to make place and invited him silently.

He felt that the accused, whose head was bowed, was peering intently at the young man in the witness box.

He saw him when he turned his head. There was neither fear nor shame in the narrowed eyes, the clean-shaven, heavy face. It looked completely wooden.

The man seated next to him pointed out the defense counsel who was behind the desk at the western end of the room. He had a sprig of *tulasi* tucked behind his ear, sacred ash smeared on his forehead and tired eyes. He looked at the old man vengefully, full of disgust.

He had heard stories about his legal triumphs. The man had retired after saving many criminals and more money than he needed. And he had come back now, to save the enemy!

When he was walking back through the grounds of the court, someone had stopped him.

'How is the case, Sir?'

'It's going on.'

'Swami is clever. Will he get him off?'

'Who knows?'

'He should be let off. Then we'll take care of him.' Who had said that? Hate had blazed in the eyes in the pock-marked face.

'The court might let him off but we won't!'

He wanted to say, 'Moideen, I'll be with you to see that.'

An appeal, a petition for mercy. He had arranged for news to get to him regularly. The week before, a friend in the court had come and told him that the date had been fixed. The eleventh of March. In the morning.

He had been telling himself ever since he started: Suleiman, I am coming to see your face as it awaits death.

The town which was well-known for its central jails and the children of white men's concubines. Krishnankutty told the driver the way.

The gate set in the huge wall was wide open.

Vasu said: 'The quarters are on the other side of the road. Do you want to take a look? We can call Jamal if he's there. He's a friend of mine.'

'No, I know the Jailer.' Krishnankutty got down from the car.

They came to the second wall.

Vasu said: 'The sanctum sanctorum. Hindus call it the garbhagriha.'

Sentries with bayonets stood in arched niches on either side of the massive iron gate. As Krishnankutty talked to them, he sat in the car looking at the enormous steel door. He knew Krishnankutty would talk too much. Don't you know who's sitting in the car? Abdul Razack, the famous ...

The small barred door set within the steel shutters opened.

'You can go in, Sir.'

He had to bend to enter. The door had been made small so that you had to bow down before the might of the law. He had heard that there was a board saying, "For each man what he deserves," in front of the Nazi concentration camps.

On either side under the high roof were two raised platforms with a small corridor between them. Guards off duty sat talking to one another on the cement platforms, smoking.

There were stairs going up on the left side. Krishnankutty spoke to the handsome guard standing there. They were given permission to go up.

There were only two chairs in the Jailer's office. A bell was rung for another chair and while they waited, Vasu made room for himself on the bench heaped with papers. 'I'll sit here.'

A dark-skinned, middle-aged man in coarse, faded khaki shorts and a loose vest made of the same material brought another chair. As he was leaving the officer said:

'Rama, ask them to send up four cups of tea.'

The Jailer said to them as the man left, 'He's a lifer.' Then added, in case they had not understood: 'A life sentence. Seven years are over. He has one more year.'

They listened, although they knew these things. When convicts have been imprisoned a long time and are thought to have mellowed, they are appointed as orderlies.

Vasu had a doubt to clear: 'Excuse me, Sir, don't these people have checked uniforms?'

The Jailer laughed. 'Only in the movies!'

He went on in an aggrieved voice: 'No one knows anything about our jails. People like you should come and look at them now and then. Things have improved quite a lot. Good food. Measured in grams. Mutton twice a week.'

He was amused. Welcome, my friends, welcome. Tasty food, good exercise. Come, everyone!

'In the Student Congress Movement in 1942 ...'

No one paid attention to Krishnankutty's experience of jail. There were footsteps on the stairs. He looked at the face of the dark-skinned, middle-aged man as he placed the glasses of tea on the table. The veins above his jaws moved as if he was chewing something. There were little circular bald patches between the stubble on his scalp, the scars of sores.

The Jailer said, as we drank tea, 'Suleïman Moopan is here. The hanging is tomorrow.'

He felt a lump in his throat. He swallowed the tea with difficulty and said without showing any interest: 'Oh ...'

'The murder case created quite a sensation in your part of the country.'

'Yes, yes.'

'What was the victim's name?'

He sat silent, rubbing his eyes with his fingers as the Jailer tried to recall the name.

Krishnankutty came to the forgetful officer's help.

'Do you want to see Moopan?'

The companions on either side of him must have exchanged meaningful glances.

'Yes, we do.' He added, by way of courtesy: 'If you don't mind.'

'It's a pleasure.'

The Jailer locked his table, got up and pulled his khaki shirt down.

'We'll walk around.'

When he walked past to go out, he saw the long, thin, red gash across his right cheek that looked as if a sharp thorn had grazed it.

'Come, I'll introduce you to the Superintendent.'

The Superintendent was in the next room. There was a board with his name and designation on the door.

The Assistant Jailer went in and talked to him, then invited us in.

A grey-haired man with a gentle face and gleaming eyes was seated behind the table. I thought to myself, didn't this man look like Ayyavu Iyer, the Mathematics teacher in the Orphanage High School?

When the introductions were over, he said: 'I thought we'd just step in and see you ... we were passing this way ...'

'Very nice of you.'

The Superintendent handed over the heavy bunch of keys that had been hanging on a large ring on the wall to the Jailer.

As they thanked him and moved out, the Jailer asked, 'Would you like to see the gallows?'

He looked at his companions for a moment.

'Yes, if you don't mind.'

The Superintendent took out a key from his table, opened the iron safe in the corner of the room and took a long key from it. He watched the Jailer take it from him reverently with some amusement.

The Superintendent smiled and said: 'This key is one of the things in the jail that we guard very carefully.'

The sunshine had dimmed. Everyone in the narrow office rooms upstairs and in the verandah was sweating profusely in the heat.

We walked past wooden shelves piled with coarse garments and went down the stairs.

The orderly moved aside to let us pass.

He asked the Jailer as he walked beside him, 'What was his crime?'

'Raman's? A double murder. His wife and her father.'

Walking by the edge of the garden at the end of the courtyard, the Jailer fondled the crotons that stretched their heads out through the wire fence and said: 'All this is the work of the inmates.'

He talked incessantly as they went through the weaving shed and the workshop. Assuming an expression of deep interest, he walked beside him. The inmates wove all the clothes they needed. Our carpentry section is a leading one. We supply furniture to all the schools.

Old grey buildings stood stooped inside the squares marked off by wire fencing.

He saw the prisoners crowded together in the grounds near the banana grove. When the Jailer drew near, they raised their hands silently and saluted him.

'They've all committed major crimes.'

They stopped at a spot where four paths branched off and the Jailer pointed out the hospital and the recreation room. He was gasping for breath. A row of young coconut palms above the roof showed off their full clusters of nuts proudly. He looked at the group of criminals. As the guard called out a number, each of them would move two steps forward, salute and repeat it.

The Jailer followed his glance and said: 'Did you see that old man? He's from Koratti. The fair-skinned stout one is a teacher. He murdered his wife. Look at that young man—no, not that one, the one behind the fellow with a moustache. He's the one ...'

The Jailer told them the story of how the man had killed his elder brother right in the middle of the road, taken his severed head straight to the police station and surrendered.

'Don't you want to see the kitchen? Come, come, that's a must! We give our inmates a larger ration than they would get outside.'

They saw a machine consisting of two receptacles, one inside the other, compress cooked rice into flat cakes. The Jailer asked for one of the cakes to be broken up and spread on the floor.

'Isn't that enough? What do you think?'

The Jailer told us about the old man working in the kitchen as we left. 'He was a troublesome fellow when he arrived. There was not a day when he didn't come to blows with someone. But after four or five years, everything mellows, doesn't it?' He laughed.

An empty dormitory. Raised cement platforms that served as beds. He remembered nights in the orphanage dormitory. At the head of each cement platform, above the rolled-up mats, calendar pictures of Hindu gods and the crucified Christ were stuck here and there.

On the way back, they saw prisoners bathing in open cubicles with low walls. The murmur of voices they had heard at a distance died down as they drew nearer. They could hear only the sound of water from the taps falling on the ground.

When they passed the hospital and the empty B-class rooms for prisoners and came to the banana grove on the south, he lighted a cigarette. He did not ask if it was allowed. The Jailer was talking about an incident that took place in Salem. A man had gone out in the evening with his wife for a walk. A prisoner who had just been released after serving his sentence stabbed him with a *bichuva*, a sickle, from the back. Fortunately he was wounded on the face, not on the neck.

'The people caught him. He was given five years—but in Coimbatore.'

He said with a sly smile, 'In four or five months I too got a transfer to Coimbatore.'

'What was his reaction when he saw you again?' asked Vasu.

Running his index finger over the thin red line that time had transformed his wound into, the Jailer smiled. 'Wasn't that why I worked so hard for six months to get a transfer? I know how to deal with tough fellows.'

He grew silent for a while, as if thinking of something.

'They understand only one language. And you can be sure it's not love!'

Yes, I understand.

He would have thought of his assailant, lying in the hospital. Then, when he finally received his transfer orders from Salem and caught sight of him in the distance, working in the labour ground, his heart would have filled with joy.

I too understand.

They walked on until they came to another gate in the wire fence. There was a small open ground in front, dotted here and there with withered bushes. They saw the huge globe of a light on the iron pillar in the centre. There were tiled buildings on both sides. Barred iron doors opened into the verandah.

'Cells for the condemned prisoners.'

A shudder ran through him when he heard the Jailer's voice.

He took another look. In the single cells, behind the barred iron doors, he could make out human figures.

'There are seven of them. Three of them are in the mercy petition stage.'

As we entered the courtyard, the guards on duty in the verandah saluted the Jailer.

The Jailer was replying to Krishnankutty's queries. The hanging was at four in the morning. That's a convention ... yes, yes, definitely ... I have to attend. Let me see.

I? Yes, quite a number.

He stood looking at the withered grass on the dry ground and at the base of the iron post.

'There, there, Suleiman is in number three.'

He summoned a mask of courage to his face and turned his eyes that way. The third door. The murderer, Suleiman.

He hurried behind the Jailer to avoid looking at the people who stood saluting behind the first two doors and climbed into the verandah.

He felt a sense of weightlessness in his trembling ankles. Someone seemed to be trying to break open the bars inside the cage of his heart.

'Well, Suleiman, do you know these people?'

'Razack Master, isn't it? We come from the same place.'

He tried to smile, standing next to the Jailer in front of the barred door. Moopan, under whose feet the earth used to tremble when he walked. The stubble on his face was overgrown and the face itself looked small. He looked completely changed.

Moopan smiled. One of his front teeth was broken.

The words he had thought up for this moment eluded him. He clasped and unclasped his fingers that were trembling helplessly and tried to smile. Moopan stood smiling behind the iron bars.

The Jailer said in a low voice, 'He is well-behaved. Very brave.' This was not a picture of the enemy—it couldn't be. This figure in the loose, coarse vest, the tapering shorts gathered at the knees, the broken tooth showing in a smile—it was so different from the one he knew.

'Master, is everyone well?'

Words still eluded him.

'Do you see Raghavan Nair? Are Rajettan and the others well?'

The words came at last with difficulty.

'Yes.'

'How's Mammukka's business?'

'Not bad.'

'Tell them all that I enquired about them.'

He saw Krishnankutty's face and Vasu's on either side of him. And heard the stillness with which they held their breath.

'Will you go back today?'

'Yes.'

'I'm so happy you came Razack Master.'

Silence spread around them again. The Jailer glanced at the empty cells on either side. The scraping of the sentries' shoes standing guard in the verandah was the only sound.

He read the mute appeal on his companions' faces. Let us go.

'I have people in Ponnani,' said Suleiman. 'They've agreed to take away the body and do whatever has to be done.'

The Jailer explained: The body would be handed over if there were claimants. Otherwise the burial could be arranged here.

The questions he had meant to ask lay silently in his mind. 'Why did you do it, Moopa, why?'

He said, with great difficulty, 'I'm going, Moopa.'

He held out his hand. When the rough palm extended through the bars lay in his, he did not think of the fingers in his blood-stained dreams.

Moopan asked: 'Won't it do if you leave after ... the ceremony in the morning?'

He did not look at Moopan's face.

He had always prided himself on the wealth of his language, but he fumbled for words now. And said, feeling helpless:

'Have courage, Moopan.'

He withdrew his hand slowly. Moopan looked at his own hand for a moment, then pressed it to his forehead and said:

'My salaams ... to all of you.'

For the first time, he heard Moopan's voice tremble and the sound of a sob that he could not control.

He stepped down from the verandah into the courtyard without waiting for the Jailer. Voices murmured salaams from behind the iron bars.

He thought, I am no one. No great man with the power to grant freedom.

The Jailer caught up with him and asked, 'Then you knew Moopan before?'

The smile on his tired face assented.

'You knew the murdered man as well?'

He replied to that too silently.

That death orphaned me—for the second time.

They were about to walk straight on. The Jailer said, 'One minute. Don't you want to see the gallows?'

Jamal, the Assistant Warden, who had come on duty at six, joined their group. He walked with Vasu a little behind them, talking softly.

They walked westward, skirting the area which had single cells to house murderers moved out of the mental asylum.

The Jailer kept explaining: lights burned all night on the verandah and the courtyard outside the condemned block. The sentries could see every movement the inmates made in each cell. When the door was opened at four in the morning and the prisoner was led-out, he would be surrounded by armed guards. There were people who had run away and attempted to commit suicide.

The prisoner's arms were tied behind him as soon as he was brought out. As they were led away, some of them screamed, cried out. Some would have to be dragged along.

'... Yes, yes, it can happen. There are prisoners who have torn their uniforms to make a rope and hanged themselves. When I was in Salem ... they can't do that anymore ... did you notice? The ventilators are very high. Besides, the guards can see what is happening inside right through the night.'

They stopped before another wall covered with moss. Heavy wooden doors with iron hoops.

'The gallows are here.'

He peered beyond the wall. When he was young, the mention of the gallows had always brought to mind the image of a machine that looked like a huge crane in the harbour, visible from every point in the jail. But all he could see here was a roof of faded tiles above the moss-covered wall.

The lock was wrapped tightly in cloth. Jamal unwound the

cloth carefully. The Jailer took out the long key from his pocket of his trousers and opened it. Pushing open the doors with difficulty, he reminded his assistant: 'Jamal, see that these hinges are oiled.'

It was dark inside. Shut away from sunlight, the air was dank and humid and had the odour of decayed flowers.

The Jailer, who could see even in the dark, turned on the light. In its faint yellow radiance, they saw before them the engine of death.

Consciousness faded into a kind of twilight. Words seemed to be crawling somewhere into the distance.

'There are executioners in the Poojappura Jail in Trivandrum. From families who are hangmen by tradition. Here we have to do it all ourselves.'

'How long will it take?' Was that Krishnankutty's voice?

'Simple. Here, Mr Razack, stand beside me. Look here, they are made to stand on this platform. The rope is slung from this beam. I'll show you.'

He took out the cord from the whistle on the shoulder of his khaki uniform and tied it to the crescent-shaped groove on the iron arm.

'This is the noose. Jamal, pull that lever. Look. Yes, when you operate the lever with your foot, the platform opens downwards like the twin panels of a door. Below, there's a pit ...'

There was silence around the machine. They followed the Jailer. He said with pride:

'In Poojappura, it is the executioners who make the rope. Here, we have it specially manufactured in Madras. It's very smooth. The executioners make rougher ropes. It takes longer.'

They saw the steps leading into the dark pit.

'Do you want to go down? There are steps.'

'No.'

'Two or three minutes. By the time you go down, it's all over.'

He gave them details, anxious to convince them how

efficiently it was done. 'Very simple. As soon as they are brought in, the head is covered with a hood.'

Then he gave them figures. About … three minutes to bring them here from the cell. One minute to cover the head with a black hood, stand them on the platform and operate the lever. Altogether … altogether everything would take about six or seven minutes.

'The body can be collected from that door.'

'Let's go,' he said to his companions, loud enough for the Jailer to hear.

'One second. Want to hear a joke? Last time—when was it, Jamal? The seventh. When we went down to the pit to look at the dead body, there was a snake there.'

'Wonderful!' he murmured.

'What?'

'Perfect arrangements.' Excellent planning. Bright lights in the yard and on the verandahs. High ventilators. Food tested and declared poison-free by expert doctors. Smooth ropes specially manufactured by mills in Madras …

He exclaimed, sounding almost intoxicated with pleasure: 'Beautiful! Wonderful!' Then he turned towards the door fighting for breath, trying to hide the sobs rising in him.

He bent down and went through the wicket gate, shook the Jailer's hand, trying hard to smile and thanked him again.

As the car turned, they saw, between the high walls, the gravel path meant for the vehicle to go to the rear of the gallows and collect the body.

They drove the fifty-six miles back to the hotel on the seaside in silence. He got down and said goodbye to his companions in a monosyllable.

He tried to forget the hours creeping by amidst the crowd and bustle, the drunken, meaningless words.

When he collapsed on the bed, the clock was striking two.

Darkness thick as granite slabs closed in around him. A deep sleep almost like unconsciouness descended over him like a pall of black.

When he opened his eyes, struggling to breathe, he was startled to see his wife's frightened, tearful face.

He heard her voice, drenched in tears: 'What is it, what is it?'

His neck was being crushed. Holding it tight with both hands, he wept and said, pressing his face into his pillow:

'It was I who died, it was I who died.'

Red Earth

The granite slabs were still burning from the heat of the midday sun. The group of visitors hastily discarded their footwear and ran into the shelter beyond the large door.

He took a long time to remove his shoes. So she stood waiting in the afternoon sun, like a solitary flower in the last green patch left by the vanishing spring. She waited, feeling the heat from the granite slabs run up her bare feet. She had felt a thrill when the rough lips of the burning granite had first pressed against the cold soles of her bare feet. The thrill turned into an agonising pain which she tried to bear quietly. She laughed to herself recalling her new-found ability to talk to herself silently. Goddess Parvati had done penance amid the five fires. Is there a *pativrata*, a chaste woman, who cannot bear the mellow heat the noonday sun belches out?

He finally managed to get out of his shoes, wiped away the sweat gathered in the folds of his face and hurried towards her. But she would not go forward.

'Come, come, my feet are burning.'

He walked hurriedly into the temple so as not to be isolated from the group. She still lagged behind. She could hear the guide's echoing voice. A voice that matched his figure.

'In the distance, at the point where the three oceans meet the Goddess sat in meditation. From here in Suchindram the Lord saw the Virgin Goddess and was filled with love for her.'

On his forehead the sandal-paste mark had almost been washed away by sweat. She imagined he had been a demon's statue sleeping on one of granite blocks, that he had now come alive to join the tourists. His eyes, in which red veins stood out with clarity, strayed from face to face as he mouthed his well-memorised sentences.

Her companion tried to persuade her to join the group while she hung back. He read what was written on the boards at the base of the enormous figures and repeated it to her as if to a child.

'The Gods felt that the Virgin Goddess would lose her divine strength if she wed. They decided that the marriage should be prevented.'

Sweat glistened on the bare granite-like body of the guide. She recalled the sorcerer who had come in her childhood to their kitchen to melt down lead in order to perform an exorcism.

She pretended to identify the names on the boards when she realised that he was watching her through his thick glasses to see how she reacted.

'They decided upon the auspicious moment when the marriage rites should be performed, the hour of midnight. The Holy Sages could agree only upon that moment as the most auspicious. Lord Shiva, the bridegroom, set out to reach the point of confluence of the three oceans at the appointed time. Devendra came in the form of a cock and stood in his way and crowed. Thinking that the auspicious moment had gone by, Shiva returned disappointed.'

'Then what about the Goddess?'

The visitors turned round to look at her. She was surprised: was it she who asked that question?

'Look here; look at this.'

Whenever he spoke impatiently bubbles of spittle would come out through his lips.

'Then what about the Goddess?'

The red-veined eyes of the guide reached out over the visitors and hovered on her. The blood-red eyes were laughing.

'The Goddess snapped the wedding garland and threw away

the pieces. She tore the pandal apart. It is because the dishes made for the wedding feast that day soaked through them and changed their colour that the sands of Kanyakumari are red.

'Come, come here.'

He called again, open camera in hand. There was a foolish grin on his fat face as he beckoned to her as if asking her to come to a secret love tryst.

'Let's take a photo with this background. It'll be good. There, stand there. Move a little to the left; let me see.'

The visiting group had reached the Dance Hall. The echo of the guide's voice boomed. He was describing the windows that had been made so that the lovely women of the household could watch a performance without being seen themselves.

'Laugh, just once. Smile please.'

She looked with terrified fascination, over the heads of the tourists, at the face of the demon with the blood-red eyes.

'Ready. Smile please. Ready.'

She turned when she heard the click of the camera.

She saw the thick lips trembling and the disgusting white bubbles of spittle gather at the corner of his lips. He was always like this when he tried to conceal his anger.

She burst out laughing.

'You did not laugh then. You always laugh at the wrong moment.'

She had moved away and he found himself talking to the stone elephant with the granite ball in its mouth. She could not help laughing again.

The tourists trooped out. Some of them tipped the guide. Before she could say anything, he muttered: 'Money for this! Everyone knows these things.'

He found a seat quickly on the bus. She looked up at the upper deck of the vehicle. She sat on the extreme edge of the vacant half of the seat, taking care not to touch the brown shirt soaked in sweat.

The bus filled up. Their former guide climbed in as the whistle blew. He stood in front of them gripping the iron bars in his hand. Her companion seemed to have thought of something and, as if to amuse her, he said: 'You've only heard of the Negro. You can see one now.

She could not see the eyes with the blood-red veins running through them. He was gazing into the distance somewhere.

Her companion watched her feet beating time to the tune the young man in the front seat was playing on a mouth organ.

When they had gone far enough to hear the roar of the sea he asked, 'Tired?'

She nodded. It could mean yes or no.

'I have always liked the sea. We went to look at the sea when I first came to your house with your elder brother for the vacation. Do you remember?'

She sat with her eyes closed.

'You remember nothing. Not even the first time I saw you!'

She tried to smile.

'We all went together. You were a child then. You wouldn't remember.'

She looked silently at the trembling fronds of the palmyra trees on parched earth receding into the distance.

'You wouldn't remember. You were dressed in a long white skirt which trailed on the ground and a green blouse. Your sister was wearing a saree. You wouldn't remember.'

I remember. You walked down with the waves holding *chechi's* hand. You took her photograph. You wiped away the drops of water that the waves had splashed on her hair.

'You didn't step into the sea. You were afraid.'

I sat in the shade of the coconut palm. I wrote on the sand with my finger; "Sri Rama is a thief." I wrote it again and again. I thought a big wave would come to wipe it out and engulf you all. What I had written remained. No wave came splashing up.

When they saw the seat in the distance he said, 'Oh! How beautiful!'

'Who? My chechi?'

'What—Oh no, the sea.'

People who had come to see the sunset crowded in little groups here and there. They move their way back through them. By the time they reached the hotel he was panting.

She did not pay any attention to the directions he was giving the servant boy about the luggage. Twisting the window curtain fluttering in the breeze, she looked out at the sea. Red earth!

When they were alone he asked, 'These needless comments about your sister ...'

'I didn't say anything.'

'You'll never finish saying it. That's my affliction!'

His face reddened with an infusion of blood. Sweat streamed down in channels. She opened the suitcase and took out the bottle of tranquillisers. She dropped two pills on his trembling hand. He swallowed them and drank some water. Short of breath, he lay down on the bed.

As she changed her saree and started powdering her face she realised that his tired eyes were questioning her.

'I'll go for a walk.'

At the door, without turning back she repeated, 'Take rest. I'll be back after a stroll.'

She saw the guide sitting by himself on the cement bench on the path beside the sea. Although there was another path opposite, she took the one next to the bench. The Negro stood up suddenly like a demon with his head touching the sky. He joined his palms, 'Namaskaram!'

A voice that boomed; the penetrating odour of country liquor; his eyes were red flames. She paid no attention to him and tried to look as indifferent as she could. She walked on, her head held high against the breeze.

She sat on the edge of the path looking at the sand dunes in the distance and the red streaks in the sky above. The seashore was growing deserted. She dreamt of the pandal that was once put up there. Around her she saw scattered on the ground the decorations that had been torn apart, the ornaments that had been broken and flung away, the food that had been kicked over and stamped into the earth.

She was afraid to turn around and look. She had to find out whether there was a light in the window of her hotel room. Even if it was not to see whether the drunken demon seated in meditation on the cement bench had waken up.

The crunch-crunch of sand being stamped underfoot. The demon approached, the beedi tip glowing like a third bloodshot eye. The emptied seashore trembled beneath his feet.

Behind him, the light from the hotel room brightened. She pressed her elbows on the red sand and raised her face to the darkened sky. She listened attentively to the sound of the heavy feet sink into the sound as they come nearer and nearer. She lay with her eyes closed, as if all her strength had drained out of her.

Once Again in Search of a Refuge

Yet another journey in search of a refuge.

The river, again.

Long ago, there used to be a travellers' bungalow at the bend of the river, where it turned towards the village. The picture that memory drew held a heap of empty tar barrels at the edge of a yard overgrown with grass. The profusion of red flowers clustered on the oleander trees in the background reflected the rays of the setting sun even on the east. Long ago.

Looking at the spot from afar, the twilight red of the oleander flowers was missing. He could see the river at the turn of the path. What month was it? The days and months of the Malayalam calendar had dropped out of his mind long ago. There was water in the middle of the river. Below him, the ferryboat had left for the other bank. He was delighted—he had once grieved to see the river become an expanse of burning sand.

The ruins of the old temple lay among the overgrown thickets.

What was the name of those plants with tiny thorns and pale pink flowers that looked like ear-studs? He used to know their name, these plants that served as a fence. He had crept through them often, holding the thorns away from his body. My plants, he thought, my months, my times for transplanting seedlings ...

He walked down the road along the river bank. A

government jeep came from the opposite side. The red earth road had been tarred. There was no dust. A bus crowded with people going to the village overtook him.

Had he missed his way? The banyan tree was not there. The stone bench meant for resting headloads was not there either. There were no stray goats reluctant to come out of the fields at dusk.

Someone in the group watching the ferryboat crossed to the other side, came up to him and asked:

'Has Anita gone?'

He did not know what to say in reply. Who was Anita?

'There's no K.B.T. Someone said Anita would come a little early.'

It took him a few moments to realise he was talking about a bus.

'I don't know.'

He walked on, passing more unfamiliar faces and reached the small bazaar at the second bend of the river. It was then that the eastern sky growled. He waited near a shop which was closed and listened to the indistinct sounds. He heard low rumblings again in the sky.

'The northeast monsoon now, in the middle of the month of Vrischikam?' An old man gazing at the eastern sky asked, maybe of nature. No one answered, nor did the old man wait for a response.

The small lane grew dark. There were isolated lamp posts now and street lamps, but no one had lighted them. Pale flickers of yellow light gleamed here and there in the thatched rooms that served as shops.

He stepped onto the open verandah of the closed shop and leaned against the wooden planks. People walked in and out of the shops on either side, taking no notice of him.

He decided to walk on. Where did this road end? Tell me, where does this end?

He used to know, once. But the road had changed now. The river had changed. The faces had changed.

Three or four people who passed by in the gathering

darkness stopped and turned to look at him. They came up to him hesitantly.

He heard one of them say, it's a stranger.

'Who is it?'

He mumbled something indistinct.

'Where are you going?'

Without waiting for a reply, one of them said, there's no bus today.

He recovered a lost voice and words: 'I need a place.'

A place.

They stood aside and talked to each other in low voices. Then came forward.

'For strangers to stay ...'

There was silence again.

'There are no hotels here. It's not a town.'

'There's a travellers' bungalow four miles away.'

'It's full. I asked,' he said. Was there something peculiar about his voice? They seemed to be waiting wonderingly for his next word.

'What I want is a place to rent.'

'For how long?'

'For a few days. I can't decide by myself for ... for how many days exactly.'

Along with curiosity, there was a tinge of respect now on the villagers' faces.

'You didn't tell us what you do.'

Instead of answering, he made a vague sound.

A man who looked capable and confident came nearer. His narrow eyes pierced the darkness as he looked at the bag on his shoulder and asked:

'Your things?'

'They'll come.'

They began to whisper among themselves.

Disembodied voices.

-Must be the Salt Inspector. Must tell Kothamma to be careful.

-Oh no! Must be a C.I.D. chap. That case ...

-He's a stranger. Can't be trusted. These expert burglars nowadays
-Would thieves be so bold?
The villagers came nearer.
'You insist on a house? If it's a day or two …'
'I must have a house.'
The walls of a house around me. A floor to sleep on. Under the sky above, a small roof.
'Only the Eman's, the Master's, house is vacant. His manager just left.'
'Who's Eman?'
They were surprised.
'You don't know Dharman Mudalali? What a thing!'
Dharman. He had never heard of him. Appu, Appa, Appunni, Kutti Narayanan, Kutti Sankaran. The old names had changed.
Who was Dharman?
'You must have heard of the Master.'
He grunted, a sound that could mean anything.
'There can't be anyone who's not heard of him. He's so prosperous.'
Someone brought a lamp. From a shop nearby someone else brought an old bench that could seat two people.
'Please sit down'
He sat down and listened, showing no interest at all, as if they were talking about accommodation for someone else. Someone had seen the manager coming out from Chitran Tirumeni's outhouse. The first messenger they sent came and reported that he had told him about the matter. A little later, another messenger came, drenched in perspiration and said: 'He'll come. The manager will come.'
Then he didn't need to see Eman?
'You can see him later.'
The locals took the visitor's side and listed the shortcomings of the village. If strangers came, there were no hotels where they could eat. No place where they could sleep. The travellers' bungalow was always occupied by revenue or government

officials. That was not all. There was the Anita bus service. There was not a day when it ran properly.

An unexpected question assailed him:

'Are you on duty, Inspector?'

He looked down and laughed silently from inside his sweat-stained, faded clothes. Inspector. Supervisor. Overseer. The villagers changed his position from time to time. They had all come to investigate. They were searching for unknown paths on soil that had changed its very face.

The villagers spoke for him, made efforts on his behalf.

And he waited.

It was not new to him, this kind of waiting, for someone who would come and tell him where to turn at a crossroad he did not know. And now he waited for a manager who worked for an owner he had never seen of a house he might rent.

A mongrel came running up from the south and sniffed at the people around. Then it came up to him, stood there uncertainly and ran off northward.

The manager came at last. He would have to face a lot of questions again ... The fear that he would have to fumble for answers was unfounded. The manager hurried towards him, taking long strides, his hurricane lamp tearing apart the darkness on the road. The knot of people moved away to show him respect.

The manager said to everyone there: 'I've got the key.'

They expressed their wonder: 'Really? We knew only you could pull it off.'

'He'd shut the place up after the village headman left, saying he wasn't going to rent it out anymore. How many people asked for it! Would he listen? Your things ...?'

The villagers answered: 'They'll come.'

'It must be infested with bats and mice and bandicoots upstairs. The ground floor won't be too bad.'

The villagers said: 'One person doesn't need much space.'

'When the things come, will the coolies know the way?'

He did not answer.

The villagers came to his help.

'We'll arrange with the shopkeeper here.'

Good.

He followed the glow of the manager's lantern. Four of the villagers went behind him. Someone chased away the mongrel that came sniffing at them again.

The paths cutting across the fields were wet. There were rumblings again in the dark sky. The darkness that had run away from the pale light of the open fields hovered in the yard they entered and in the locked house.

In the dim light, he made out the wooden door which had once had carvings on it. The manager opened it with an effort. The hinges creaked in pain.

'Wait. There must be a lantern inside.'

The manager went in with his hurricane lamp. There were sounds of more doors being opened inside. Then the stairs creaked. The manager brought out another lighted lantern and placed it in the porch.

'Your things?'

The villagers repeated: 'They'll come.'

'What about food?'

'I had some on the way.'

'The well is there,' said the manager, pointing it out. 'The bucket is by it.'

After what seemed to him like a very long time, he was alone. The dark house, the smoking lantern and the rusty key were in his possession.

He blew away the specks of wood falling down from the moth-eaten ceiling and lay down, his head on his elbow, gazing into the darkness outside.

The manager had promised to come again the next day to discuss the rent and other formalities. A vague meeting in some faraway space called tomorrow. Forget it, he thought. He had finally found a house. Bats upstairs, white ants which had eaten into the worn wood downstairs, crickets outside. All the same it was a house, the refuge he had imagined during his wanderings. Yes, my friends, a refuge for me as well.

In the morning, people gathered in the first teashop to open in the bazaar, to find out about the stranger who had just arrived. They waited for the manager to come and see the new tenant. It seemed he had not haggled about the rent. He had paid it in advance saying he did not want to be in debt. He was going to engage workmen to clean the house.

The manager went on. Our Eman's a loner. And harmless. But he's quite mad at times. Sometimes he'd say he didn't want any tenants, sometimes that he wanted to demolish the house and rebuild it. Sometimes ...

The villagers agreed: 'The Master's always like that!'

People hovered around the rented house without going in. To see the new person who had come from another place. The yard had been cleaned. Workmen were planting karaveeraka saplings to form a higher fence at the edge instead of the old broken one. Watching the new tenant wring out the rag with which he had mopped the floor and spread it out to dry, they asked, hoping to strike up an acquaintance: 'Have your things come?'

'They have.'

He was relieved to see them go away with a satisfied smile. They had not asked when the things came or how.

He worked hard. He had to clean the cobwebs before the next batch of villagers came. And chase out the bats.

The workman who had gone to the market arrived with provisions and household articles.

When the palm leaf screens over the windows were lifted, light poured into the house. The musty odour of stale air slowly disappeared. He walked in and out of the house with a faint air of possessive pride.

The memory of the room he had slept in when he started on his journey had grown dim. He tried to recall it as he lay down, tired after working late. Pots of wet clay turning smooth as they rubbed against the spinning potter's wheel. The smell of burnt clay in the kiln. Fresh clay moulded in various shapes everywhere he looked. A floor smeared with cowdung. In the direction where drains filled with the stench of urine snaked towards the light, only smoking kilns could be seen.

It was from that room that he had started his journey. Over the years his footsteps, wandering over fallen leaves and dust, had left no impressions. After that—verandahs leaking with rain water, bamboo screens and benches stained with sweat and dirt, interminable paths, nightmares ...

In the evening, he planted the rose cuttings the workmen had brought in the corner of the yard. He arranged the new pots and pans in the room that darkness had vacated for him. He gazed wonderingly at the pan boiling over the lighted fire.

At night, a lighted lantern and the Eman's manager arrived, cleaving the darkness.

'You're well?'

'Yes!'

'No trouble of any kind?'

'No.'

The manager expressed doubts about the wisdom of having the yard and compound cleaned. A place that belonged to someone else. If the Eman told him to, he would have to vacate. The manager advised him not to waste money.

When the manager left, he told himself confidently, I won't vacate, I won't give up the house.

He made friends with the people around. He could identify the yellow birds in the clump of bamboo near the fence. The little birds that pecked at the grass around the areca nut trees began to recognise him. What a wonder, weaver birds began to build a nest in a corner of the western room. One night he discovered that the chirp of the crickets in the fields had a rhythm of its own.

Once the villagers who came asked him:

'Have you decided how long you want the house?'

He said calmly: 'I am not leaving.'

They were shocked.

Someone who knew the Eman and the manager said: 'All the beams are rotten. It seems they want to rebuild the place.'

He grunted, concealing his uneasiness. Someone said:

'It's a place no one wanted. Now that there's a tenant, Master's being difficult!'

Before the rains came, the manager came and told him. The Eman is not going to thatch the roof. He says, let it leak and fall down.

The manager was reluctant to accept the advance rent. But he insisted on giving it.

The rains started. The wind whistled over the fields, then blew through the areca nut palms. The showers grew heavier and rainwater collected in the drains. The areca nut palms and banana plants shivered, completely drenched by rain.

He sat inside and watched fearfully as the rainwater seeped in through the cracks in the crumbling mud walls and gushed into the house. Was everything going to collapse, just like the owner wanted? Straw blew off the verandah. Water that was stained red poured through the gaps in the roof. He went out in the rain, made a paste of clay and water and tried to block the cracks in the walls. He lined up pots and pans on the floor to catch the water gushing through the roof. He mopped up the water that the wind had driven in.

Then the furious rain stopped. The last puff of wind lingered in the air like a child's whimper.

The manager came again. He did not smile or sit down. He wanted to say to this man who wore such a stern expression, look, I've plugged the leaks. I'm going to repair the roof. I'll see that this old house doesn't collapse. I'm not vacating it.

The manager sat there looking as if he was annoyed with someone, while he went out and called workmen from hutments in the next compound. They plucked leaves from the palmyra tree near the fence and thrust them into the gaps in the roof.

Sunshine still wet with rain spread around them.

The manager said without looking at him, holding out the balance of the rent: 'The Eman says you have to leave the house. Here, take this.' He did not take it.

'It's not my fault. That's Master's nature. He won't listen to anyone.'

The manager left the money on the seat and walked off. When he got to the gate, he turned.

'It's better you go. What else can you do? No one has ever gone against Eman's wishes.'

The villagers came. They would not look him in the eye either. But there was sympathy in their faces.

'We're sorry you're leaving. What can you do? It's the Master's house. You have to leave when he tells you to.'

The manager came again three days later. 'They're sending people to throw out your things and evict you. I don't know anything. I'm going.'

He went to the small inner room and bolted the door.

They would come, Dharman Mudalali's hired labourers.

He did not light a fire. Through the window, he could see the paths across the fields. He pulled the window shut.

He heard the lowered voices coming nearer and nearer and asked, with a start:

'Who is it?'

They were Eman's workmen.

He did not say anything. He swallowed hard.

He heard the sound of pots and pans being hurled out. Then the sounds of the house being broken up.

'We have nothing against you. We're doing what the Master told us to do, that's all.'

'We're tearing down the roof. Then we'll break the walls down. We'll smash the walls of the room you're sitting in last of all. You can sit there till Eman comes.'

'Will he come?'

'He will. If he says he'll come, he will.'

Another period of waiting. He peered out through the window. Pots and pans were scattered over the courtyard. Things he had collected on his travels. The fields were still empty. Perhaps ... he made a wish. That the Master would change his mind.

I will call him Yejamanan, Master. I'll always call him that. I'll prostrate before him. Look, give me back my refuge. At least this final refuge that I found. I can't bear it. Travellers in soiled clothes, waiting endlessly. Rooms reeking with the odour of dirty bundles and sweat. Cold benches. The smell of burning kilns. I can't, I can't go back to them.

Muttering to himself, he paced the room within the four walls that still stood.

Look, clay-stained rainwater will no longer flow through the gaping roof. The rain and wind will not come through the palmyra thatch—just look.

He lay down, warning himself to stay calm. When the evening light faded, he shivered. Was darkness creeping in on him like the Yejamanan?

There was no place to run away to. Where were those sounds from? Were they hooves or human footfalls? Were they cattle returning home? He waited, a bundle wrapped in a filthy cloth clutched to his breast.

Somehow, when the fearsome sounds came nearer, he did not feel afraid. Heavy footsteps, coming up the front steps, then into the verandah.

He placed the bundle quietly on his head, closed his eyes and lay down. The doors wept as they were opened, showing the way in.

Come, Yejamanan, come.

The Sale

He had more or less learnt the topography of that huge city. It was not difficult to understand the instructions given on the telephone. He got off at the bus stop near the Siddhi Vinayaka temple, asked a few discreet questions to make sure it was the road leading westward to the seashore and walked along. When the woman's voice had asked on the telephone whether he was coming by car, Sunil Roy had said he was coming in a taxi—and accused himself of an unnecessary shred of false pride.

Any instructions given to someone coming in a taxi were of course applicable to those who came on foot as well. The soft voice of the woman had said in convent-accented English: 'A kilometre after you come on to Sea Face Road, you will see a high-rise building under construction on the right side. No one can miss it. There are large flats coming up there. Another five minutes and you'll see this building. The name is Sagar. Remember, Sagar. It's flat number nine on the fourth floor.'

'Your name?'

'That's not necessary. Flat number nine, Sagar.'

Since she was selling household goods, maybe a shred of false pride prevented her too from revealing her name.

It was farther than he had expected. Most of the buildings had names associated with the sea. Large old buildings in spacious compounds full of trees and ornamental shrubs. Finally, he saw the skeleton of a huge building with many floors on his right. There was a big crane on top of it, the labourers underneath looking like so many ants. He walked on and saw Sagar exactly where it should have been. If people had to be given directions, they had to be as accurate as this.

It was an old building. There was a Gurkha watchman on the ground-floor verandah, half sitting, half reclining, leaning on his elbow, looking very bored. He moved slightly and looked at the visitor, but said nothing.

The lift had gone up. He pressed the bell and waited. He could hear the machine creaking and groaning as it moved, tired of going up and down the spine of the old building. A middle-aged man with patches of leucoderma on his hands and lips opened the door and stepped out, a suitcase in his hand. Sunil thought he resembled Gopal Dutt, the cashier in the first newspaper office where he had worked.

When he got off at the third floor he saw three doors in front of him. Number nine was right in front and there was no board outside. Maybe the names of the residents on all the floors were displayed downstairs. He should have taken a look. In the science of buying and selling, it was useful to address a person by name. He thought of his old Sales Manager's study class. It was because he could not master that science that, fed up after five years of selling sewing machines, Sunil had gone back to the love of his youth, journalism.

He pressed the doorbell. Was he being inspected through the magic eye on the door? The small corridor outside was dark even in the daytime. Those who looked from inside would not see anything clearly.

As he wondered whether to press the bell again, the door opened slowly.

'I phoned a while ago. The name is Sunil Roy.'

The door opened fully. In front of him was a tall, slender woman in a blue saree with a touch of grey in the strands of hair over her forehead. Her very fair skin seemed to have a tinge of yellow.

'Please come in.'

It was the voice he had heard on the telephone.

'My God!' There was a sudden note of anxiety in her voice. 'Did you step on it? Did you?'

She bent down and picked up something. A small paper packet.

She explained: 'They're flowers for the puja. The maid servant usually brings it in. You didn't step on it, did you?'

'No.'

He followed her in.

'Just a minute. Excuse me. Do sit down if you want to.'

She opened a door on the right of the living room and went in. That must be the master bedroom. Was the master of the house performing a puja or having a bath?

How ugly the building looked from outside! And yet, once you were inside, the flat was beautiful! The venetian blinds had been pulled up and one of the shutters of the glass window lay open. A cool sea breeze blew in through it. The leaves of the money plants growing in brass jars swayed in the breeze.

Until now, Sunil had had only a vague idea of how to furnish a flat if he were to live in a big city one with someone of his choice. Here was an excellent model before him.

A sofa set upholstered in black leather. A carpet in the centre. A big heart-shaped glass-topped table and small round stools with little cloth covers on them. He looked for the price of the set. Maybe it was not for sale.

The experience of the two Sundays previous to this one had taught him that the articles for sale in large houses were usually kept aside. Cards with the price written on them would be hung on each piece, to avoid bargaining. You could take a look, buy if you wanted to or walk out.

He realised that she was not performing a puja inside but wrestling with a cupboard. To the right of the door through which he had come in was the kitchen. Its counter opened into the living room. Food could be picked up from the counter and passed onto the guests. The visitors would not see the ugly faces of the kitchen or the servant. It was not enough to have money, one had to know how to live in style: that was one of Father's golden dictums. Father had been contemptuous of the newly rich. He had derived the greatest amusement from decrying them. Even in his last days, when he did not have the money to buy the opium he needed to relieve his suffering, he would describe the courage he had displayed, wearing khadi when going for an interview before an English Sahib. While struggling to live on the salary of the forty-five rupees he earned as an elementary school teacher, he had secured a first class in the B.A. degree examination of the Calcutta University. He would talk of all this repeatedly to his companions.

The mistress of the house came back and said:

'One of the cupboards doesn't open. What a nuisance!'

As a matter of courtesy he asked: 'Have you lost the key? Is it for sale?'

'This is the key all right. I opened it even yesterday.'

'Can I help?' asked Sunil hesitantly. Not many people knew that this was not an act he put on: helping women, being at their service, had become a part of his character. Therefore little things he did were often misinterpreted. They would say it was not chivalry but chauvinism. Gowri went to the extent of calling it a masked male chauvinism.

'Please, will you?' She gave him the key.

'My husband sent in this advertisement just the day before yesterday. And then he had to go on a business tour. It's I who am in trouble now.'

She opened the bedroom door and showed him the cupboard. Sunil noticed the new air-conditioner. The key was bent because she had used force when the door would not open. He made an effort to open it, praying he would not fail.

'Sorry. It won't open.'

'Never mind.'

'Is there anything you need urgently in …?'

'No, nothing like that.'

They went back to the living room.

The telephone rang. She picked it up and gave her number.

'Yes, that's right. Come and have a look. To tell you the price of each … come and look at them, that's best.'

She put the telephone down and said: 'Now all sorts of

bothersome people will come and nothing will be sold. He put in the advertisement without telling me. Now I have to talk to everyone who comes. There have been telephone calls since six thirty this morning.'

Sunil Roy reminded her of what he wanted.

'The things for sale?'

'All these. The sofa set. The dining table. The bed. Everything's for sale.'

'You're leaving Bombay, are you?'

'Ahmedabad next. A promotion and transfer for my husband. What are the things you want?'

Sunil thought for a minute.

'The ad mentioned a typewriter.'

'Oh, that's gone. A man in this building came in the morning—actually, the servant from the next flat. His brother types petitions for a living. Poor chap!'

He wondered if she had given it away out of compassion. He thought unhappily that if he had started out as soon as he had read the *Times*, he would have got it cheap.

'It ... it was the typewriter I wanted.'

'It was a very old machine. He bought it when he got his first job.'

He was not interested in anything else. Still, for the fun of it, he asked: 'What will this sofa set cost?'

'This.' She thought for a while, scratching the top of her right ear. 'I wonder where that paper's gone ...'

She began to search for it. She said, 'I know, we should have noted down the prices on tags and hung them on all these things. That would have saved trouble for the buyers. But I didn't think anyone would buy anything. When I reminded him about the ad just as he was about to leave yesterday, I saw him scribble something on a piece of paper.'

She finally found the piece of paper between the pages of a book.

'Here it is. Let me see. Sofa set ... four thousand.'

He concealed his surprise.

'It was made to order when we were in Calcutta. We must

have spent much more than that. Still, will anyone buy it for four thousand? I doubt it. It's far too much, isn't it?' She spoke haltingly, slowly, then suddenly very fast.

'Isn't it?'

He essayed a smile. 'I think so.'

'Mr Parekh, my husband, thinks all this looks old-fashioned now. You're not buying it anyway, are you? Don't they all seem brand new?'

'They certainly do.'

'Are you from Bombay?'

'No, from Calcutta.'

'A Bengali?'

'Yes, Madam.'

He saw a sudden eagerness in her face.

'I like Bengalis. Most of my friends, my close friends, are Bengalis. And Calcutta—it's my favourite place. Whatever people might say, Calcutta is the best place in India. What does this Bombay have ...?'

He tried to smile. He remembered Calcutta had dealt him its share of wounds. He had arrived in Delhi, believing it was an escape. But that city too had not been behind the other in dealing him wounds—through his newspaper office, through Gowri. This was his third city.

'I've only been here three months.'

'You'll soon realise. Wait a bit. Bombay will suck the life out of you. Look, it was after I came here that my hair began to turn grey.'

She smoothed out the strands of grey above her forehead.

'They say those who have stayed in Bombay never want to leave it. I would be happy to run away even a day earlier. What's Ahmedabad like?'

He admitted his ignorance. 'I don't know. I've never been there.'

'I'm sure it will be better than this. My flat in Calcutta— how peaceful Lake Road was.'

He decided to offer a deserving word of praise:

'Isn't this a pleasant flat? The sea just beyond and a cool breeze.'

The telephone rang.

As she muttered, 'This nuisance will go on all day,' and walked to the phone, the doorbell rang. She appealed to him: 'Please!' Then said in broken Bengali, 'Must be a buyer. Please talk to them on my behalf.'

Was she using his mother tongue in order to take liberties with him? He was amused. Was the man who had come to buy an old typewriter going to play the role of the man of the house?

He opened the door and saw a short man with glasses in a white safari suit and a stout woman who had vermilion smeared thickly over the parting of her hair. Upper middle-class, he thought. Husband and wife. Maybe married couples began to look like each other over the years.

The husband asked in English, with no trace of a North Indian accent, 'Is this the place mentioned in the advertisement?'

Behind him, Mrs Parekh was describing the household articles. He thought the person on the other end of the line must be the sort that was insistent on knowing all the details.

He put on a salesman's smile and said, 'This is the place. Come in and see. Welcome.'

'What are the things?'

Drawing a half circle in the air that took in the sofa set and dining table, Sunil Roy said: 'All these.'

Mrs Parekh burst out laughing over the telephone. Covering the mouthpiece, she said to him in Bengali: 'When I said a thousand rupees for the bed, he asked what was so 'is-special' about it! Does he want to know whether there's something else that goes along with it?'

He had no desire to laugh. He invited the visitors into the living room.

Mrs Parekh spoke into the telephone again: 'I was laughing with a friend of mine. Come and have a look and buy it if you like.'

The woman who had come asked: 'You are Bengalis, aren't you?'

He nodded in assent. Their attention was on the dining table. An oval one that would seat eight. The chairs had high backs and carved legs.

'How much is it?'

Mrs Parekh moved to his side so that he too could look at the piece of paper in her hand. It was quite hard to read Mr Parekh's handwriting. A dining table, then 'eight chairs' in brackets—he was embarrassed to tell them the figure written against the words.

Mrs Parekh ran her index finger under the line. There were traces of nail polish on her fingers. She prodded him silently.

He said, 'Six thousand.'

The woman looked at the man with a twisted smile, as if she had just heard a joke.

The man gave Sunil Roy a look that seemed to bore into him and asked: 'Really?'

Since he did not want to admit defeat either in his role of salesman or as the temporary master of the house, he said very seriously: 'It's new. It was made to order a year ago. How much do you think it will cost to make a set like this now?'

It was the woman who replied. 'You may be right. But one comes to a sale to get things cheap.'

The husband asked, looking as if he was ready to listen to another joke: 'What do you want for this sofa set?'

With her eyes on the paper, Mrs Parekh raised the sum: 'Five thousand.'

He looked at her and realised she had not said it by mistake. The husband and wife moved to a corner of the living room for a whispered consultation, then came back. The woman took out a visiting card from her handbag and held it out to Sunil, saying:

'Our card. Please call this number if there is any change in the price of the dining table.' She smiled at Mrs Parekh, inclined her head and walked out, followed by her husband.

He looked at the card. Mr and Mrs Dharadher. Both were doctors with foreign degrees.

Mrs Parekh read the card and said: 'Doctors ... with their own clinic. Must be making plenty of money. With both being doctors, I wonder what their family life is like. They cannot hide any of the secrets of their bodies from each other, can they?'

Not able to find a direct answer, he said vaguely, 'Who knows?'

To make sure his role in the drama was over, he said, 'I'll go now.'

'Sit down,' she said. 'You spoke in an authoritative tone, like Mr Parekh. It's a godsend that you thought of coming here. I would have gone mad if I had been alone in all this confusion.'

He sat down on one of the seats near the glass window. On the seashore below, washermen were washing clothes on the granite slabs scattered here and there. The sea seemed to peer in at this point and go back. The expanse of blue tinged with black was calm. The line of water where the inner sea met the ocean seemed to him to have a metallic gleam.

As if to justify his sitting there feeling so relaxed, he said: Such a beautiful view.'

'Oh, it was the flat on Lake Road I really liked. I was never bored even if I was by myself for days. I've never been afraid in Calcutta.'

'What does Mr Parekh do?' he asked with a secret hope that this would be the beginning of an acquaintance with someone in a high position.

'He's an executive in Brett and Company. He'll soon be the Indian Director.'

He had heard of women of this class falling in love in order to escape the boredom caused by a combination of prosperity and laziness. Most of the stories took shape from malice. But he knew at least one artist who had made capital out of such a situation. Vipin, whom he had met in Delhi. The man had known well that even at forty-one, his face was lack-lustre, drained of blood and energy. Sunil took firm hold of his thoughts which had begun to run wild, trampling on the dead leaves of memory.

'What are you doing here?'

'Journalism.'

If she asked anything more, he thought he would tell her

the name of the newspaper whose management had agreed to consider his appointment at the beginning of the next month.

The bulge in her stomach was out of proportion to her tall, slender figure. When she stood beside him, he guessed she was at least an inch taller than he. Fifteen years ago, eyes that failed to conceal admiration and envy must have followed her every time she walked into a gathering.

'Where do you stay in Bombay?'

'Sion.'

'I've only heard of it. I don't know where it is.'

He hoped he would not have to tell her lies about the dark, unventilated room on the first floor of an old building that belonged to a grocer, next to a cemetery.

'You live with your family?'

After a minute's delay he said, 'No, alone.'

'Do you need anything else? A cupboard or a dressing table? There's a good writing table. Come, I'll show you. I had forgotten about it.'

She opened a door and he walked in. Another bedroom. It showed signs of having been used until very recently. A good writing table and chair. A number of old books lay on the table and prints of Abba and Osibisa were stuck on either side. A plastic board warned: 'A genius at work. Please be silent.'

He asked with a faint smile, 'Who is this genius?'

'My daughter. This was her room.'

'And now ...?'

'She's in London. She went there on a scholarship to study business management. Then she married and settled down there.'

'You've only one daughter?'

'Yes.'

'When you are bored with Bombay, you can go to London for a change, to your daughter.'

He thought she had not heard him. And found fault with himself for asking her about things that did not concern him.

'Who knows whether she's in London now or somewhere

else! Her last letter was about the man she was going to marry. It's a year now. We had just arrived here.'

'Who is her husband?'

'A German. She had sent a photograph. It must be somewhere here.' There were a few books in the cupboard in the room. And a landscape of some foreign country on the wall. 'She was brilliant as a student. First rank, first prize in all the quiz competitions. Four hundred candidates wrote the exam and there were two scholarships. Deepa got one of them. Do you like the writing table?'

'It's good. But I doubt it will fit in my study.'

'Take it if you like it. Don't bother about the price. It's not on the list. Let it be of use to someone. Take it.'

She wrote "Sold" on the table with her finger in bold letters and signed below. The letters and signature showed clearly on the dusty wooden top. Sold.

Sunil Roy did not show his astonishment. The telephone rang again.

'I must sell all these off somehow, then get some sleep,' she muttered as she went out. He followed her.

He asked himself why he was hanging around here needlessly. And found the answer himself: he had escaped the bleakness of another Sunday of roaming around the streets in the area.

She was describing the sofa and dining table over the telephone.

'No, there are no electrical appliances. No, not that either.'

The doorbell rang again. Mrs Parekh stretched out her hand and signalled to him. He opened the door. A young man and woman who reminded him of married couples or lovers in advertisements. Both wore faded jeans. On the young man's bare chest was a tiny anchor on a gold chain. She came in with her hand on his shoulder.

Mrs Parekh put down the telephone and said softly: 'Show them around. I didn't offer you anything to drink. Tea or coffee?'

'Thank you, nothing now. Come in, please.'

'This is where the advertisement ...'

'This is the place.' Once again, he shook off his irritation at having slipped into this situation and donned a salesman's persuasive role. 'This is the dining table. And the sofa set. The four pieces on the other side go with it.'

'Do you have a cot?'

He looked at Mrs Parekh, ready to say, 'No.' She said, 'There's a double cot. And two singles. Come and see.'

This was certainly not the young man who had asked over the phone if there was anything special about the bed. This new bridegroom or lover was pretending a greater seriousness than was needed, probably to appear more mature than he really was before his companion.

He invited them to go with Mrs Parekh.

The young man tapped the double bed with his hand. The girl pressed the mattress down. She asked half in jest,

'Will you give us the mattress with the bed?'

'Of course. You can take the lot.' Mrs Parekh signalled to him to come out.

'What should I say they cost together? There's no price marked on the mattress.'

'Do you want to sell it?'

'Mr Parekh had decided to sell everything. And change all the old things.'

She laughed softly. Her voice trembled slightly: 'I'm the oldest.' The young man and woman had come out and were waiting anxiously to know the price.

'Two cots, two mattresses, pillows: two thousand five hundred for all of them together.'

She glanced at Sunil Roy as if to confirm she had calculated right. He turned his face away.

'It's far too much,' said the girl.

He wondered whether he should start a sales talk and the young man said:

'It's not that the price is too high. What we meant is we can't afford that.'

Mrs Parekh's face brightened.

'Right. You liked them?'

'Yes.'

'Will they do for you?'

'Oh yes, certainly.'

'How much can you give me?'

They looked at each other. The girl said: 'Five hundred now. The rest in six instalments.'

The young man corrected her: 'Not six, four. Four at the most.'

'If we can finish in four instalments …'

'How much would that be totally?'

They were not the only ones to find Mrs Parekh's question surprising. Sunil Roy wondered how people could leave for Ahmedabad with debts they had to collect here. The young woman mustered enough courage to say with a smile:

'A thousand five hundred. That's all we can afford.'

Mrs Parekh said: 'Bring the money. And a truck or van. Offer accepted.'

The young people looked relieved, as if they had achieved a great thing.

'All right.'

As they moved towards the door, Mrs Parekh said, 'You must take them away quickly. With four Bombay Mills sheets as a bonus from me.' She heaved a sigh of relief as they left.

'A sale at last. May it be useful to them.'

She hurried inside as if she had suddenly remembered something, picked up a lipstick from among the cosmetics scattered on the dressing table, opened it and marked on the three pillows lying on the double bed: Sold. Sold. Sold. The telephone rang again. 'Please answer.'

He agreed to her request and picked up the phone.

'Eight-three-four-two-four-two?'

'Yes.'

'Yes, it's we who put in the ad. He hesitated a moment when the caller asked who was speaking, then answered: 'This is Mr Parekh's house.'

He followed Mrs Parekh's example and gave them a list. He invited them to come and have a look whenever they wished.

When he put the phone down, she said: 'It was God who sent you to me. God is with those who have no one of their own.'

He was beginning to enjoy this. He moved one of the stools to a spot where he could get a better view of the sea and the breeze blew better, and sat down.

'Tea?'

'No.'

'A drink? There's beer, whisky and gin here.'

He was embarrassed. 'So early? No.'

'With your permission.' She opened the cupboard near the dining table and took out the bottles. She poured out almost half a glass of gin, added cordial and took a large gulp. Glass in hand, she came and sat down facing him.

'Come on, talk. Say something about Calcutta.'

He smiled. 'What can I say? I lived there twenty-eight years. That's all.'

She gazed at some distant point in the sea and slowly sipped her drink.

He observed her attentively without her being aware of it. Dark shadows under her eyes. A moistness at the corner of her eyes, as if a drop of liquid had melted there. Her blue veins stood out on the fair skin of her arms. She looked at him suddenly and, to conceal his embarrassment, he asked:

'When will Mr Parekh be back?'

'Maybe tonight. Maybe tomorrow. He said he would call. Anyway, we managed a sale.'

She drank what was left of the gimlet in her glass, then said: 'His theory is that I do not have the capacity to do anything well. Not even to keep the servants in order or maintain laundry accounts.'

She stopped. He felt the gimlet had given her a sudden sense of well-being. Gazing at the sea, she asked: 'Which country would you reach if you went straight across the sea from here?'

It was the Arabian Sea. On the other side of it ... he tried to draw a map in his mind and failed. So he said: 'I don't know. Africa, perhaps ...'

'One should be able to cross over to the opposite shore whenever one wants, shouldn't one?'

He laughed.

Mrs Parekh looked at her empty glass and said: 'I grew up under the thumb of a very, very orthodox father. Even eggs and onions were forbidden in the house. After my marriage, when someone forced me to drink a gimlet at the first dinner party, I threw up. My husband scolded me when we got home that night for not being used to such things ...'

He looked at the shadows under her eyes as if to show that he was interested in the story of her life.

'Now he quarrels with me because I drink in the daytime. What is there to do in the daytime? Sit down doing nothing, then sleep a lot. Dinner parties at night.'

He moved into the role of an advisor and said, 'You can do a lot of things. Social work. Or you can take up a job.'

The doorbell rang again.

'I'll go.' She said as she was going out, 'Pour out another drink for me. Now you can have one too, can't you?'

He got up. But was not ready for a drink himself.

The newcomers were a bent old woman with a huge swelling on her neck and a small girl.

Mrs Parekh began to speak in Hindi and the old woman said in English: 'I am Mrs Kamath. This is my granddaughter.'

What she wanted was the sofa set. She walked around it, examining it attentively. Sunil was convinced that the old woman had seen much in her life. Her walk, her look, her speech, all of them showed remarkable self-confidence.

She used to live abroad. Her three children were abroad. She had lived with each of them in turn and was now back in Bombay. There were tenants in one half of the family house. She was going to stay in the other half.

Mrs Parekh said, 'My husband had marked the price at four thousand. I don't want four thousand. You can have it for three thousand five hundred.'

The old lady had a beautiful smile. Not one of her teeth was bad. 'Isn't that too much?' It was him she asked.

Mrs Parekh smiled. 'Auntie, what's your budget for a sofa set?'

The change in her attitude was obvious.

'I don't have a budget to speak of. The tenants give me some money. And I still get a bit of my husband's pension.'

'Still, there must be a figure in your mind.'

'No, there isn't.'

The old woman sat down on the sofa. Mrs Parekh sat down beside her, took the child by the hand and made her sit down too. She laid her hand on the old woman's shoulder and said softly: 'Auntie, that's a mistake. A mistake we women make. We don't have a budget for anything. No estimate, no accounts. That's why our men have to go to such trouble.'

She looked at Sunil Roy as if to ask whether she was right. He was confused, not sure what she had in mind.

Mrs Parekh continued to talk to the old woman and her granddaughter. 'Our men lose heavily in business. They lose at the card table. Their pretty secretaries land them in losses. None of this hurts their valour. But if we don't maintain our household budgets, they'd be shattered.'

There was a smile of sympathy on the old woman's face. Mrs Parekh took the child's hand and said to her affectionately: 'You must learn this when you grow up. Don't forget.'

Sunil Roy made his decision. To make up for lost time—what had he lost?—he would help himself to a drink and then leave. He walked to the liquor cabinet with his empty glass.

Mrs Parekh was talking very softly to the old lady, who seemed to be protesting from time to time. She took the old lady's hand and said something that sounded as if she was pleading with her. He heard the old lady say as if she was in a trance, 'Thank you dear, thank you, dear.'

She took her grandchild's hand and left.

He was immersed in mixing his gimlet. Mrs Parekh came up to him looking very happy. 'I've sold it! Nice old woman. I hope she keeps well and has many guests.'

He was about to add cordial to her gin but she gestured to him not to. She added some water to it herself, raised the glass and said formally, 'Cheers!'

'How much did you sell the sofa set for?'

'Don't ask. It's sold. It wasn't nice of us to have sent those doctors away. Where's that card?'

She began looking for the visiting card she had left on one of the stools. He swallowed a mouthful from his glass lest it spill over, went up to the window and looked out at the sea. Another meaningless day was creeping past him. He wanted to talk to someone. He had not come across a single friend who was worthwhile the last three months. It was then that he saw it—the huge advertisement on a page of the women's magazine lying open on top of the curio cabinet. Gowri, modelling a saree, with a bewitching smile. He felt no animosity towards Gowri for having escaped from the prison of wifehood she had been in with the senior subeditor Sunil Roy. Had Gowri's smile really been so bewitching? Gowri had become more beautiful when she became a model.

He was halfway through his drink when he heard her voice, delighted at having found the lost visiting card. Mrs Parekh picked up the telephone. 'Dr Dharadher?'

'Then put me on to Mrs Dharadher please.' She winked childishly to signal that the person she wanted was coming on the line.

'This is Mrs Parekh. What price can you offer for the dining table you saw? Tell me ... don't hestitate.'

The reply must have come after the other person thought it over for a while.

'Agreed. Come and take the things. You're welcome.'

She put the phone down and said, 'Grand! Simply grand! It's sold. The doctor is happy.'

He took out the crumpled packet of cigarettes he remembered having in his pocket. Luckily, there was one left. He lighted it and looked out at the sea, savouring the flavour of the gin.

Mrs Parekh came and sat down again facing him. A mild excitement coursed through his veins.

THE SALE | 95

He wondered whether to talk about Gowri. He did not want anyone to tell him Gowri had been in the wrong. All he wanted was for someone to say *he* had not been in the wrong. Some disinterested third party.

Mrs Parekh said, 'You must come again. Even if we are in Ahmedabad. You're a journalist after all, you'll be paid for your time. You can interview Mr Parekh and write about him. Won't it make a good story, how a mere salesman rose to be a director?'

'All successes make amazing stories.'

'What is there left to sell? Please stay until everything goes. I'm alone, don't you see? It was God who sent you.'

'This sale ... is it one of the amusements of the wealthy?'

His voice was quite serious.

'We have to sell everything and vacate the flat,' said Mrs Parekh, paying no heed to his question. 'Perhaps you can go to a little more trouble for me and do me one more favour?'

He was willing to hear what it was.

'Even after everything is sold, people are sure to keep coming. I will lie still on the floor here. Write some kind of price on a tag and tie it around my neck.'

He tried to smile and failed.

'It's not a joke. What figure will you write? You look to me like an intelligent person. What price will you mark? Tell me ...'

He did not say anything. She leaned against an arm of the sofa and said, 'I didn't sleep last night. I could not sleep even after I took three Calmpose tablets. What price will you mark on the tag around my neck?'

The doorbell rang again.

Mrs Parekh said without opening her eyes: 'Sell anything you please. At whatever price they offer.'

He hurried to the door. It was a tall, lean man, with a skin as fair as a foreigner's. His moustache had been blackened with an eyebrow pencil, he had long, thick hair with a tinge of grey in it and blue eyes. There was a briefcase in his hand.

Sunil closed the door and the newcomer looked at him in surprise. Sunil said: 'This is the place. A cupboard, a sofa set and ...'

The man asked: 'Who are you?'

Mrs Parekh sat up on the sofa. 'Welcome. I am Mrs Parekh.' She pointed at Sunil Roy and said, 'That is Mr Parekh. We are selling all our old things and going in for new ones. She prodded her own chest with her finger: 'You can name a price for everything including *this.*'

Sunil thought the visitor looked stunned.

Mrs Parekh began to laugh softly. The laughter grew louder and louder, became interspersed with sobs.

The visitor crossed the room in three or four quick strides, gave Mrs Parekh a sound slap on her cheek and said in a low voice:

'Learn to behave yourself. To behave.'

The laughter ceased and there was silence. The distant murmur of waves hovered outside.

Seeing another Sunday which had begun with faint expectations coming to an end, Sunil Roy opened the door quickly and went out.

He checked outside the door, to avoid making a mistake. Was there a packet of flowers? No, there wasn't.

When the Doors of Heaven Open

Kutti Narayanan could not help thinking how ill-fated a river was if the water in it should flow waist-deep even in the month of Thulam. If this was the situation now, the villagers were really going to suffer. But then, in all houses these days, men and women had begun to bathe in closed bathrooms. Even the Christian chap from the pump-house, who used to come to bathe in the river at this time, was not to be seen.

He finished his bath and was drying his dhoti in the breeze when Thami the cheruman came with a message: 'They've asked you to come at once. To Madhavan Thampuran's.'

The old man must have something for him to do. Maybe he wanted an offering to be made in the temple on the other bank of the river. Getting there was easy. Only three and a half miles. But the return trip! If it was an auspicious day, by the time the puja was over and he collected the *prasadam*, the sand of the river bed would have turned burning hot. He could not wear sandals because of his corns. And when he came back after the walk over the hot sand and gave the old man the prasadam, he would subject him to a spate of advice. He would remind him of all the sins he had committed on various occasions in life. Then, out would come twenty-five paise with a flourish, as if he was doing something great. It had in fact become a ritual to receive Madhavan Master's advice, his reprimands and the twenty-five paise.

Kutti Narayanan was annoyed to see Thami waiting on the river bank. The cheruman stood there as if he had brought a warrant of arrest to take him away.

'Get going, rascal, I'll come.'

'They said in the house that the Thampuran is worse.'

So he had been sent from the ancestral house. Couldn't the stupid fellow have told him earlier? A feeling of happy anticipation spread through him. Careful not to show it, he said, 'Walk along. I'll come straight there.'

So the schoolmaster Madhavan Nair's time had come at last. He made a mental calculation. Eighteen years older than he was. Master was seventy-two now. Seventy-two was a ripe age to die.

Kutti Narayanan was the most helpful man in the village of Kizhakkemuri. He was in demand wherever there was a birth or a death, a twenty-eighth day ceremony after a baby was born, the day a child was fed rice for the first time or during a wedding. Formerly, it was Kottilil Chathu Nair who had conducted these functions. It was he, Kutti Narayanan, who had attended Chathu Nair's death. But in Chathu Nair's time, customs and traditions had been strictly followed. Nowadays, when labour pains began, there was no need to send for the village midwife. Even the women of Kizhakkemuri had their babies in nursing homes. Wedding feasts did not have to be supervised. Were there men now who were bold enough to conduct a wedding in their ancestral home? Weddings were held in the Guruvayoor temple. There were no rituals for death anniversaries, no elaborate funeral rituals, no ceremonies for feeding a baby rice for the first time. All that remained were deaths. And even those were few.

As he wound his half-dry *mundu* around his waist, he made a mental calculation. It was a good thing Madhavan Master had decided to die. It must happen after sunset tomorrow, he thought. If he gave his relatives and near ones the chance to arrive as he drew his last breath before sunset the next day, it would be auspicious. There would be the right configuration of the zodiac signs: the conjunction of the eleventh and twelfth days after full moon, with the Thirovonam star in the ascendant. The moment when the doors of heaven would open.

There were only three of his children to come. His sister's children were right here. Since his children lived in distant places, the miserliness which was characteristic of the folk of Kizhakkemuri would not have affected them greatly. They would give generously when they left. It would be no empty boast to say no one knew as well as Kutti Narayanan how to make a person die neatly. There were rules for deciding when to close the eyes, when to tie up the mouth and so on. And then, it was no small matter to bathe and lay out the body and smear *vibhuti* on it. When Kutti Narayanan laid it out, smeared with vibhuti, the body would take on a dignity of its own regardless of how disreputable the dead person had been.

True, on days when he had nothing to do, he had to put up with the barbed words people threw at him. It was all his fate.

He had been a pupil in the fifth standard, the class taught by the Madhavan Nair who was awaiting death now. You learnt much more writing and arithmetic in those days in the fifth standard than the B.A. students of today did. When all the older members of his family died and he was left alone, he stopped studying. That was when he went astray. He had inherited land which yielded a modest quantity of paddy and fifty cents of areca-nut garden. He learnt to gamble. Since he found farming tiresome, he leased out the land to tenants. Then, maybe because the stars that presided over his life were unlucky, he developed a liking for the taste of toddy. It was because he was ill-fated that he was pushed into evil ways.

When he finished a bath in the river, he usually stopped by Kunhuamma's house, took a pinch of vibhuti from the basket hanging on the verandah and dabbed it on his forehead. Today, he felt he was entitled to go right into the verandah. Kunhuamma's daughter was nursing her baby.

'Where's your mother?'

'She must be around somewhere,' she said without looking at him.

Kutti Narayanan said solemnly, 'Call her.' Kunhuamma came out just then with a winnowing tray full of paddy.

'Kunhu Kutti Amma!' he cried, adding the word 'Kutti' as a mark of respect. 'Madhavan Nair is finding it difficult to breathe. I'm on my way there.'

Kunhuamma said philosophically: 'All of us have to die one day or the other.'

'I have to organise things there. Won't get even a drink of water until all the rituals are over. Give me a glass of good water.'

Although extremely miserly by nature, Kunhuamma fell into the trap. In the old days, Kutti Narayanan used to take a little ground sandal paste along with the vibhuti to smear on his forehead. She had complained that he was wearing out the lump of sandalwood and hidden it! The way she had brandished a broom and driven out her husband was another story. Kunhuamma felt unusually kind-hearted towards Kutti Naryanan, on his way now to preside over a man's death.

'Hey, children, give Kutti Narayanan a glass of tea. And two idlies if there are any.'

Kutti Naryanan waited, chanting his prayers. He called out to those inside: 'Whatever it is, bring it quickly. Everyone there will be confused, not knowing what to do. It's only at times like these that we can be of help.'

Three idlies came with the tea. They did not taste too good, the chutney had been diluted with too much water.

'I'll see you when I'm a little more free, Kunhu Kutti Amma,' he said by way of thanking her as he walked away. Smiling, he murmured to himself, 'I'm the only one who calls her Kunhu Kutti Amma. But does the black ogress show me any gratitude for it?'

Crossing the rice fields, he went along the old path bordered by screwpine bushes that had now become a road and climbed the hill. This hill, Thannikunnu, had once been barren rock. Now many houses had been put up. The Panchayat President had said a road would soon go through it.

Of late, he had been avoiding going to Madhavan Nair's,

dreading the climb. But of course he had to go if he was sent for.

The man who was about to die was a person everyone in Kizhakkemuri respected. He led a well-ordered life. He did not chew betel leaves, use snuff or smoke beedies. He had learnt about Kutti Narayanan's newly-acquired evil habits only when he saw him involved in a brawl in front of the toddy shop. Master had sent for him and rebuked him. 'What a pity! You were intelligent enough when you were a student. What's happened to you now?'

Master reminded Kutti Narayanan that he had been very good at arithmetic. People would respect a person only if he made something of himself, he counselled. What a lot of advice like this he had received at various stages of his life! All this had happened because of certain configurations of the planets. What could a small individual like him do against the planets that directed his destiny? A married life that lasted a month. Which God-forsaken hole was that bitch in now?

He was nearly at Master's house. Master was educated, a man of the world. It was his bad horoscope that had brought about his failure in life. The house was still unplastered. After the partition of the property, the kitchen block had been demolished, a bathroom and lavatory had been built for his convenience and even a small room to store grain.

During the floods the next year, the river had rushed by devouring half the garden. They had predicted heavy rains the following year as well. Yet another flood took away three quarters of the front yard. Fearing that the Flood of '99 would wash away the house itself, Master had sold the property to a Moplah Muslim for the price he named. It was the next year that embankments were put up to protect the river. They did not need to fear the floods after that. The Moplah family built steps going down to the river and could have baths in the river now like princes.

It was then that Master had built his house on the hill. By the time it had to be plastered, he had run out of money. Master stopped work on it, saying, let the children work on it at their convenience, and moved in.

There was no one to be seen. Kutti Narayanan said to himself, this is what is so special about the Kizhakkemuri folk. They're never to be seen when they're needed. Master's nephew, Achu, and the Christian chap, the Chettan who looked after the pump house, were on the verandah. Chettan had bought some land on the hillside and built a house. The man who had arrived to work in the pump house had become the owner of forty cents of land in four years' time. He wondered, would the salary the man earned for pumping water allow him to save that much?

Achu asked angrily: 'Hey, where were you? Gadding about when we needed you here ...'

'I was having a bath when I got the news, Achu,' he said and walked into the house. Achu's mother, Narayani Amma, Master's younger sister, who was seated near the bed, looked at Kutti Narayanan through her thick glasses. He thought it was Chakkama's daughter, Cheeru, who stood leaning against the wall.

Master lay with his eyes closed, breathing normally. Kutti Narayanan looked at him attentively.

'He makes out when he's called.'

Kutti Narayanan sat down beside him and stroked his forehead. He called softly: 'Master!'

'Master, it's me, Kutti Narayanan.'

Master's throat and lips moved as if he was trying to say something.

'There's phlegm in his chest, it's congested. Put a frying pan on the fire, child. Take out some rice bran and make two poultices, this size. Heat them moderately and hold them to his chest. He'll have some relief then from the phlegm.'

He said to the sister in a low voice: 'Otherwise he'll suffer when the real breathing trouble starts. Do you have Kasthuryadi tablets here?'

The sister didn't know what they had in the house. She'd arrived when she heard Master had fallen ill.

'If there aren't any, buy some. And boil some water with cummin seeds.'

He walked out.

Although Achu always scolded him when they met, the man knew his worth. Which was why he asked: 'What's his condition, Kutti Narayanan Nair?'

Kutti Narayanan thought deeply before he answered: 'Won't live to see the fourth day from now. We'll see what happens tomorrow or the day after.'

He made another calculation. 'Tomorrow night.'

He looked at Achu. Achu knew he never made mistakes about such matters.

Pump-house Chettan asked: 'Should we send for a doctor?'

'Buy some Kasthuryadi tablets when the Ayurvedic shop opens. We won't need anything else.'

'The doctor will come this way when he's going back from the dispensary. I telephoned him.'

Kutti Narayanan smiled wryly.

'Do we need the doctor? If it's to be a peaceful end, in my opinion, it's better not to poke needles into him. Have you informed the children?'

Achu grunted.

'Isn't his son in Coimbatore?'

'H'm...'

Chettan said, sounding astonished: 'He walked around the compound just yesterday. Read the paper and philosophised on things for quite a while. That's what the human condition is.'

Master lived alone. After his wife died he had spent a month with each of his daughters. Then he came back here.

He used to have a woman at first to do the cooking. When a match factory was started on the hillside, she stopped coming to the house to work. His sister began to send him food from the ancestral house, but he said he did not want it. Chakkamma's daughter cleaned the house every morning and drew water for him. As for cooking, Master managed on his own.

It was only recently that his vision had become poorer because of cataract. Master knew if he went to Thrissur or

Kozhikode and had an operation done, his vision would be restored. He postponed it because there was no one to accompany him. Kutti Narayanan had said he would go along. But Master would not have it. 'No, you won't do. Let's wait till one of the children is free.'

That morning, Master had not opened the front door even when Cheeru had finished sweeping. Chettan had arrived just then. Master used to get the newspaper every day. The last three months, he had not been able to read the small print. Chettan would read aloud to him, then Master would talk about the news. Only after this would Chettan rub his body with oil, do his exercises and have a bath in the river.

Chettan looked through the window and saw that Master was asleep. He called out, there was only a groan. It was then that Chettan sent Cheeru to bring Achu and forced open the back door with a hack knife.

'If you ask me ...' Chettan looked at Achu and Kutti Narayanan, 'he should have gone in his sleep. That would have been fortunate.'

Achu did not say anything. There had been no need for the old man to live like a hermit, cooking for himself. He could have died in his ancestral house. These old fogeys would remain obstinate to their last breath!

Kutti Narayanan did not agree with Chettan. Die in one's sleep indeed! Death, like birth, was an important ceremony in life. An event to be celebrated, conducted stage by stage. To die without all that in one's sleep was a kind of deception. All those who had done good had to go through the different stages. They *would* go through them.

Pacing the verandah, Achu lit a cigarette. He was a member of the Panchayat. And a director of the Agricultural Cooperative Bank. A very busy man.

'I have a committee meeting at ten. The Block Development Officer will come this evening. A hundred things to do today.'

Kutti Narayanan said, 'You can go, Achu. There's no point staying here. Nothing is going to happen today. Come when you're free. I'll be here.'

Achu said: 'Let Amma be here. There are phones in all the places I'm going to. If you need me, tell them at the house. Malukutty will telephone me.'

Achu had been the first person to install a telephone at home. Even now, the Kizhakkemuri folk had still not come alive to the miraculous capacities of the telephone.

Achu went in, spoke to his mother and came out. As he was about to go, Kutti Narayanan reminded him: 'Bring the Kasthuryadi tablets when you come. If you can send them earlier ...'

'Send one of the boys for it.'

Achu took out a five rupee note from his pocket and held it out.

Kutti Narayanan calculated. Six Kasthuryadi tablets cost three rupees. Three would be enough for the present.

Chettan said he would have a bath, go to the pump-house and come back at once. Cheeru said the rice bran and frying pan were ready. 'You must be here. There'll be people dropping in. We'll have to serve some of them tea. Have some boiled milk ready. Get another half-measure from somewhere.'

Cheeru's mother Chakkama came into the courtyard. She worked on building sites, carrying headloads of quarry stones.

'Who are the stones being quarried for?'

'Assanaji's son.'

'Oh, the chap who went to Dubai. Has he come back?'

'It's quite some time since he came. He'll go back now only after the house is complete and the housewarming over. There are twenty people carrying stones!'

'Go to the bazaar and tell the *vaidyar* to send five or six Kasthuryadi tablets through one of the boys. It's urgent. We'll pay them here. Bring it yourself if you can spare the time.'

Chakkamma hesitated. 'It's very late.'

The local rate for transporting stones was twenty paise per piece, but these people had made it thirty. If they started early morning, they could move a hundred stones by dusk. But Chakkamma was not one to forget that she had worked for the family a long time. That's why she had sent Cheeru to work here in spite of her complaints. No one knew it was for just ten rupees a month.

'Let me see, Master.'

'It's not enough to say that. Do it.'

Cheeru reminded him, 'The frying pan is red-hot.'

'I'm coming. Chakkamma, you can send one of the boys.'

Chakkama said, 'Who's likely to be there at this hour ...?'

As Kutti Narayanan heated the rice bran, prepared a poultice and took it in, he thought: at least there are some people who haven't stopped calling the higher castes Master or Thampuran.

Achu noticed some people getting off the bus from Palghat at the bus stop near the ferry. Yes, they were Seethalakshmi and her husband. Achu was just paying off the taxi which had brought him back from the Block Office. He got into the taxi again and said, 'Go on. I'll get down at the ferry.'

By the time the taxi reached the ferry, Seethalakshmi and Padmanabhan had picked up their luggage and started to walk on. Achu asked the taxi driver to stop, got out, paid him and walked towards them.

'There was a meeting of the Block Committee. I'm on my way back after getting them to cancel it.'

Seethalakshmi guessed the event had not yet taken place since they had met Achu on the road.

'I left the place just half an hour ago. You can't tell anything from his present condition.'

Padmanabhan asked, 'Can't you get a coolie here?'

'They've all gone to work. Give it to me.' He took Seethalakshmi's small suitcase from her. Padmanabhan walked on ahead.

'I was just starting my scooter when the neighbours said there was a long distance call. That was lucky—when we arrived at the bus stand, the fast bus was just about to leave.'

'I always find fault with the telephones for the delays. But luckily, I got through to every place I called very quickly today.'

Seethalakshmi asked as they walked along, 'Who's the doctor attending on him, Achuetta?'

'Our Govindankutty. He's quite adequate for cases like this.'

'What did he say?'

'What can he say? Uncle's quite old, after all.'

'And Vishaledathi? Have you sent …?'

'She'll come. I spoke to her. She said she'd start at once.'

'What about Ettan?'

'He wasn't there. He'd gone to the station to collect someone. I spoke to Raju and said it would be best he comes by the West Coast Express.'

Achu described how he had broken open the door that morning. Wasn't it sheer obstinacy that made Uncle live alone like this? If something had happened at night, everyone would have got a bad name. He spoke of the important meetings he had cancelled that day because of this.

'I have to run around all the time. I spent forty-two rupees on taxi fares today. Haven't you got a phone yet?'

Padmanabhan lied. 'The office allotted me one long ago. But it hasn't been connected yet. They say they don't have a cable.'

A man coming from the opposite side saw Achu, got down from the field and stood there scratching his head. Achu said, 'Kumara, I haven't forgotten about you. Let all this be over— you've heard about Uncle's condition.'

Achu wished another ten people would come one after another like this. Seethalakshmi had not had much of an opinion about the Achu who had failed his tenth standard three times and was loafing around the village. Now they wanted Achu for every little matter in Kizhakkemuri. Recommendations for jobs. How many people had this B.Sc. qualified husband of hers been able to find jobs for? Achu went around in a taxi in order to save time and be punctual for appointments. He had managed to get two ministers to include Kizhakkemuri in their itinerary and given them receptions there. And who had seen to it that Government buses passed through the village and arranged for a telephone exchange to be opened there?

As they climbed the hill, Achu asked,

'The children?'

'They have class.'

'The older one,' it was then Achu remembered his name: 'Ravi—you could have brought him.'

'He has a scholarship examination tomorrow.'

'If one of the boys is here ...'

They understood what Achu meant. It was always a son who performed the funeral rituals.

'He needn't have stayed in the ancestral house if he didn't want to. One of the children would have brought him food three times a day. That wouldn't have been difficult for them. But what can one say if Uncle wouldn't allow that?'

Padmanabhan smiled. 'Uncle is quite unique. How many times we asked him to stay with us!'

'He stayed with us just a month. He wouldn't stay with Vishaledathi even that long. Hardly three weeks. He wouldn't have liked all those parties and dinners at her place.'

'He's always been like that. Apart from some trouble with his eyes, he's never been ill.'

Seethalakshmi remembered then: 'I had written to Father last month. There's a good doctor in our place now. He did cataract surgery and restored so many people's eyesight. I'd written about that.'

Seethalakshmi's heart beat faster as they neared the house. When she went in and saw her father, she could barely suppress a sob. She sat down near Achu's mother. When she had calmed herself somewhat she asked what was happening in the kitchen.

'Don't worry about cooking anything now. They'll bring food from the ancestral house.'

Narayani Amma gave Kutti Narayanan a look as if to say she knew nothing about this. He said, 'I've arranged all that.'

Padmanabhan and Achu came in with the doctor. He felt the patient's pulse and examined his heart and chest with a stethoscope. Then he checked his blood pressure. He went out, followed by Padmanabhan.

The doctor said, 'The pulse is rather weak and the blood pressure low. There's nothing to be done now.'

Making sure they were out of earshot, Padmanabhan asked: 'What's your opinion, doctor?'

The doctor hesitated. Seethalakshmi had edged closer by that time.

'He may continue to be in this coma for quite a few days. We can't say anything with certainty. Or the end may come suddenly without any change taking place.'

The doctor was about to leave. Achu, who had been standing apart, came up to him. 'Wait, doctor.'

Seethalakshmi saw Achu put his hand in his pocket and looked accusingly at her husband. Padmanabhan took out fifteen rupees and gave it to the doctor.

'Thank you, doctor.'

After he left, Padmanabhan asked Achu: 'Wasn't fifteen enough?'

'Ah, yes ... fifteen or twenty. It's twenty for visits to the house. But in our case, it doesn't matter. The doctor stays in my outhouse.'

Padmanabhan took off his glasses, wiped them and said softly:

'Actually I thought everything would be over by the time we got here.'

Seethalakshmi agreed. 'I thought so too when we got the phone call.'

Kutti Narayanan, who was standing behind them, thought there was a hint of disappointment in both their voices.

He said with certainty: 'Wait for tomorrow night. It won't go beyond that. It's not the coma and full stop the doctor spoke about that matters. These things have a rhythm of their own.'

Padmanabhan sat down on the raised platform on the verandah and leaned against a pillar. He had thought, if they waited for Bhaskarettan, the cremation would be over by the morning at the latest. Then he could catch the direct bus at midday.

'Don't you want to change?'

'H'm...'

He knew Seethalakshmi was watching him intently.

'Kutti Narayanan has watched many people die.'

'H'm...' What was she driving at?

He asked, 'Where have you kept the suitcase?'

He went into the house with his wife.

There was an old double bed in the unused room. Padmanabhan changed from trousers into a mundu and sat down on the bed, next to the rolled-up mattress.

Seethalakshmi closed the door and took off her sari. She said, as she folded it: 'Look at it, after just two washes!'

He looked attentively at his wife as she bent down in her under-skirt to take out a mundu and *veshti* from her suitcase. It was as if he was looking at a new person. A protruding belly, full of creases. Could women change so much in fifteen years? There were very few who did not change that much. Like Vanaja. No one would guess that Vanaja, the stenographer in his office, was a mother of four. She was probably a year or two older than Seethalakshmi. He had calculated that when he saw her date of birth once on some piece of paper. Her beauty lay not only in the way she wore a sari. There was not a single crease on her belly. A body that had withstood the onslaught of age.

Kutti Narayanan called from beyond the door: 'Do you want tea? Lunch will soon be ready.'

Seethalakshmi tucked the veshti into her waist and opened the door. 'No, nothing now, we'll just have lunch.'

Sweat had formed black blotches under the arms of her green blouse.

'What did you think of him?' asked Padmanabhan.

She did not know what he meant.

'I was asking about your father.'

'What, if as the doctor said, he lies in this condition for a long time?'

She opened the window and stood facing him, leaning against the wall.

'When is the M.D. coming?'

He had answered the same question four times since they had left. He said irritably: 'Didn't I tell you in Malayalam? The day after tomorrow.'

'He'll arrive in the morning?'

'I don't know.'

She knew how important the visit was. That's why she was anxious. The Company was going to set up a new factory near Walayar. The person who would be responsible for the whole unit, the Project-in-Charge as he was called, would be nominated the day after tomorrow. Two hundred people were to be appointed for the new factory. The Project Officer would be responsible for making twenty-five per cent of the appointments from the local personnel. There would be no increase in salary—just a slightly higher allowance. But the authority it conferred ... The three kinds of pickle that were to be entrusted to the M.D.'s driver, apparently intended for the M.D.'s wife, were ready. And the special coconut oil from Guruvayoor for his mother.

'Won't he stay for a while?' asked Seethalakshmi hesitantly.

'I've asked for two rooms in the Guest House. He may leave for Ernakulam in the evening. Rajasekharan said he will not make a halt here. But he never tells the truth.'

'Can't we persuade him to have dinner with us?'

'That would be ...' He stopped, realising he had no business talking to her about office protocol. He had kept a secret to himself however. The retired I.G., Kumara Panicker, was a close friend of the M.D.'s. There would be a party for the M.D. at his house in the evening. Neither Natarajan or Sankara Pillai were ever allowed there. But he could walk in. The Black Label whisky he had sent Verghese to buy, a carton of Rothman's cigarettes ... once he knew the M.D. was not leaving, he would take them to Panicker's house and tell him: 'A relative of mine brought these from the Gulf. I have no use for either. Let them be here.'

Panicker might say, 'Good. Your M.D. is coming for dinner.'

Certain that it would not be accepted, Panicker might even extend a casual invitation.

He would reply: 'No Sir. Some other time. My colleagues in the office will say I am trying to curry favour. This is a time when so many proposals are being considered.'

While leaving, he would make an explicit offer. 'Sir, there's a cousin of mine coming from the Gulf next month. If there's something particular you would like, I can write and ask him for it.'

The retired I.G. already approved of his respectful behaviour. Nothing wrong in that. He would never repeat Natarajan's dirty tactics. Everyone in the company had heard from the Guest House watchman what Natarajan had offered the M.D. during his last visit. He had told himself firmly that even if Seethalakshmi had been younger and prettier, he would never have thought of that way.

But he had to be there the day after. It must be the authority to appoint fifty people that had attracted Natarajan and Pillai.

'I wonder whether Vishaledathi will come,' said Seethalakshmi to no one in particular.

Vishalam had to come from Alwaye. She had been to Japan the year before with her husband, apparently at the company's expense. Half the money Father had made on the sale of the house and compound by the river had been spent on Vishalam's wedding. Seethalakshmi had not realised the importance of this at the time. It was after she had had Ravi that Pangu Ettan had given her these accounts. Although Vishalam's husband had status and owned a car, it was Seethalakshmi's husband who had been of help to Father. Few people knew this. It was to Seethalakshmi Father had written when he needed a good sweater and a scarf.

Padmanabhan gazed at the thoughtful Seethalakshmi, running his fingers through his hair. He went out, stood at the door of the patient's room, took a look at him and went into the backyard behind the kitchen. The coconut palm saplings which had been planted there in pits had not yet grown and had a feeble look. Seethalakshmi followed him and stood just behind. He asked her:

'How many cents of land here?'

'I think about sixty.'

'Are there sixty?'

Master's distant relative, the deed writer Sankunni, crossed the fence at the back and came in.

'Ah, so you've come.'

'H'm…'

'I heard the news just now.'

Sankunni noticed Padmanabhan looking at the ill-grown saplings and remarked: 'Coconut palms will never grow on the hillside. They'll wither in the southern sunlight.'

'What's the price of land in this area?'

'Don't even talk about that! Koyassan sold four plots on the roadside for two thousand a cent. Isn't there a limit even for land on the roadside?'

'Wherever it's from, people have money.'

'How much would this land fetch, Sankunni?'

'This?' He glanced at the plot with the air of an expert. 'Would it be fifty cents?'

'Sixty,' Padmanabhan corrected him.

'And the house … It costs quite a bit nowadays to build a house. Maimunni's boy bought Gopi's house and compound for seventy-five. And it was only thirty cents. It's a pity the area by the river was sold for a paltry sum.'

'Will it fetch a lakh and a half?'

Kutti Narayanan came to tell them that rice and vegetable preparations had arrived from the ancestral house.

'How is he, Kuttiarana?' asked Sankunni.

'There'll be a change when the stars change their position at night. I think the breathing may become difficult.'

Padmanabhan asked, 'Are you giving him *kanji* or glucose?'

'Just a ladleful of kanji water with great difficulty. After that he couldn't retain anything.' He looked hard at Seethalakshmi to find out whether she had understood the significance of what he had said. 'It's a sign that difficulty in breathing will soon set in.'

Sankunni went in. As Padmanabhan washed his hands on the kitchen verandah, Seethalakshmi was laying the banana leaves to serve lunch, while Kutti Narayanan was washing the ladle and the flat serving spoon for rice. Padmanabhan said, 'I'll have to go to the office the day after tomorrow. I have some very important work to do.'

Kutti Narayanan thought it over. 'The day after ...' He made a gesture of helplessness. 'Can't say anything definite, Padmanabhan. The day of the week, the star, the position of the moon, are all auspicious from tonight onwards. It can take place any time after tonight. He lowered his voice and asked: 'Shall we ask Kunhikuttan Panikker to make calculations with cowrie shells?'

'No.'

'By God's grace, the rain has stopped. It was pouring when our Parakkat house grandmother died this time last year. What difficulty we had getting the firewood chopped and the body cremated.'

Padmanabhan sat down by himself to the meal. He asked Seethalakshmi, who was about to serve him: 'Where's Achu Ettan?'

'He'd said he'd go home for lunch. He has to telephone someone.'

'H'm...'

He and his phone calls, he thought! As soon as a telephone exchange came to Kizhakkemuri a year ago and Achu had a connection installed at home, he had made a long distance call to Padmanabhan's office in Palghat: 'Now it will be easy to let me know if there's anything important. Note down my number and ask Seethalakshmi to write it down at home.'

These villagers were so petty. The applications he had made for a phone in his residence had accumulated into a huge file and lay in the head office in Trivandrum. Few people knew that private companies were sometimes worse than government ones!

Seethalakshmi drew his attention to the fact that her father's sister had sent two kinds of vegetables for the meal. Well, these country folk could well afford two and three kinds of vegetables. All they had to do was pluck them from their compound. What did they know of the hardships of the salaried class?

If the death occurred after dusk the next day, he would not be able to go to the office the day after. The cremation would be over only by noon ... He could phone the office from Achu's house. If the M.D. was halting for the night, he could reach

Palghat by dusk and meet him at Panicker's house or at the Guest House. He could not be in the office during the day because of this misfortune, so it would not be wrong to go and meet him after office hours. No superior officer would reprimand an employee who was mourning a death in the family.

It would be best if it occurred tonight. Or at least the next day. If the son from Coimbatore arrived soon, they would not have to keep the body until he came.

'What news of your brother?'

'He'll come.'

Padmanabhan continued to eat. Whether Vishalam came or not was no problem. But the rituals could not be conducted if the eldest son did not come. If he was busy, he could send his son. Or his son's son. And he could come and take part in the Bali ceremonies on the seventh or twelfth day according to his convenience. Padmanabhan would not stand for the cremation being delayed because Vishalam or her husband had not come. He was ready for a row over this if it became necessary. Although he was not an executive trained in Japan, his job had responsibilities.

It was Ravi's scholarship examination that had led to all this trouble. But for that, he could have sent Seethalakshmi with Ravi. Then he could have come at his own convenience for the fourteenth or sixteenth day ceremony and there would have been no bother. When he had heard what Achu said on the telephone ... anyway, did these country bumpkins know how to speak clearly and sensibly on the telephone?

Padmanabhan felt irritated with everyone. He did not feel like eating. He got up.

In his mind, Padmanabhan congratulated whoever was in charge of Achu's kitchen. The meal had been sumptuous. This was the way food should be sent to another house. There was plenty left after three of them had eaten. After Cheerupennu ate, there would still be enough for another two persons.

Narayani Amma was lying down on a mat she had spread on the floor in the patient's room. Kutti Narayanan poured two teaspoonfuls of cummin-seed water in which a tablet had been dissolved into the patient's mouth and he moaned feebly. Kutti Narayanan suddenly realised that Narayani Amma was sixty-eight years old. She had many ailments: diabetes, difficulty in passing urine, rheumatism. Since Achu could afford it, he used to get doctors to come and examine her on and off. Narayani Amma had removed her glasses and was lying on her side with her eyes open, gazing into the darkness under the bed. Kutti Narayanan thought, as he looked at her, that she would not last long.

The sick man looked as if he was sleeping peacefully. Seethalakshmi came in and sat at the foot of the bed. The boredom of having nothing to do was evident on her face.

Kutti Narayanan picked up a fan, gave it to her and said: 'Fan him now and then. He must be feeling hot inside.'

Kutti Narayanan went out. Those who had gone home to eat had not returned. When death arrived, there would be no one around, he thought. Except those who were indebted to him. But wait and see what it would be like after Master died—the house and compound would be full of people. That was how it was everywhere. Each one would talk about what he or she had done for the dead man. When someone was dying, only he, Kutti Narayanan, was needed. The Kutti Narayanan whom the Kizakkemuri folk called a drunkard, a ne'er-do-well. It was then he remembered. Was there a copy of the *Ramayanam* here, to read at dusk? He had lost the old copy he had bought at Guruvayoor, at the eastern shrine. Cheap copies were sure to be available at the Kunnamkulam bus station.

This was the right time to write a list. If only he could get a pencil and some paper.

Sandalwood pieces: there had better be two kilos, for Master was a great man. Then six yards of mull and a length of silk, two yards. Paddy, rice, coconut oil, a wooden rice-measure: these would be available in the house. The hand-woven towels called *thorthu mundu*s were the most important item. They had to have twelve large ones. After all, Master had so many relatives.

The cheruman, Thami, walked into the courtyard. Kutti

Narayanan asked him by way of greeting: 'Don't you have work today?'

'I'm digging in the garden. How's the Thambran?'

'It's too early to say.'

He got down into the verandah and said:

'Not today. Tomorrow. But be ready. Don't fill yourself up with toddy at night and lie there dead to the world. Find two or three other people. Since it's not raining, it won't be hard to chop the wood.'

Whenever he went into the courtyard, Kutti Narayanan had always had noted the mango tree in the western corner. It was a huge one and would yield good firewood. Once the branches were bent, they would have to be bound with thick rope and pulled downwards to the north-east so as not damage the fence. He saw a woman wearing glasses walking up the hill with Achu. Wasn't that Vishalam? So the eldest daughter had arrived as well!

'We were wondering when you'd come. If you've not eaten, wash your hands and come. There's food ready.'

Achu said, 'She ate at home. She came straight there.'

Vishalam made a pretence of smiling at Kutti Narayanan and went in. Achu said,

'It's more convenient to park the car there.'

'Has she come by herself?'

'There's the driver.'

'And her husband?'

'He's gone to Bombay. He'll come later.'

'He can come at his convenience ... Master would want all the children to be with him.'

Kutti Narayanan was happy that Vishalam was in a high position. The older daughter was more fair-skinned than the younger one. She had her late mother's complexion. She had large eyes, cheeks with a tinge of rose and luxuriant hair. Although Kutti Narayanan had been afraid of Master, he had hung around a lot near the river below the house. It had been such a pleasure to catch sight of Vishalam now and then even at a distance. If only the One above had drawn a fate line that had given him a little more education ...

He went in, listened to the patient's breathing and gave him two teaspoonfuls of cummin-seed water.

Achu, who was standing at the door, said: 'The President was asking about you.'

'I wonder why.'

'I think it's his niece's engagement on Friday.'

The feast for an engagement ceremony at a Panchayat President's house would be like a small wedding feast in itself. The cook would be the Namboodiri who conducted the worship of the Goddess Bhagavati on the other bank of the river. But Kutti Narayanan would have to be there to co-ordinate everything. He had told the President openly once that though the Namboodiri performed the puja for the goddess regularly, he had stopped conducting some ancillary ceremonies, which was a mistake on his part. These were matters for which Kutti Naryanan could do something.

If the President's brother-in-law, who lived across the river, attended the engagement, a chicken was sure to be killed for the evening meal. They would have fun. An ounce of the stuff the man brought was worth two bottles of the adulterated toddy the Cherttala people sold.

'Which day is it, Achu? I hope it won't be before Friday.'

He'd be in a fix if it were the next day or the day after …

'I didn't ask.'

There was a rumour that Achu did not get on well with the President since he had been in the running himself for the office. But that was a different matter. After all, a girl was getting a husband. It was up to Achu to organise the function, wasn't it?

What if there was a crisis by dusk and breathlessness set in? It would be most convenient. If only the son would come, everything could be finished by nine-thirty in the morning and those who had come from a distance could leave in the afternoon. If he wanted, he could attend the festival in the Perumkunnath temple. The Thiruvegappura team would play the *tayambaka* on the drums.

Having stood quite some time at the head of her father's bed, Vishalam came out and sat down on the chair next to the round table on the verandah. Seethalakshmi sat on the verandah ledge.

Kutti Narayanan started the conversation: 'When will he get back from Bombay?'

'In two days' time.'

Not a strand of Vishalam's hair had grown grey. Streaks of grey had begun to appear here and there in Seethalakshmi's hair and the shadows under her eyes had grown darker. Even now, Vishalam did not look more than thirty.

'Do you want something to drink?' asked Kutti Narayanan.

'No, nothing.'

Vishalam said, addressing no one in particular: 'I thought I'd be able to go back in the evening. The maidservant is on leave and the children are alone.'

Seethalakshmi did not say anything. Noting Kutti Narayanan's expression as he gazed adoringly at Vishalam, she said irritably: 'Kutti Narayanan Nair, go and attend to whatever Father needs.'

Embarrassed, he went in.

'Edathi, change if you want to, I have clothes in my suitcase.'

'I brought a suitcase too, since I wasn't sure what would happen. It's in the car, I'll get it later.'

Vishalam raised her head up and sighed. All her calculations had gone wrong.

That morning, as soon as her husband had left for the airport, she had telephoned Yamuna although she knew Yamuna had gone to Bangalore. Balagopalan had answered. He had known the call was not for Yamuna. As though to sound convincing, she had said she had telephoned to get a recipe Yamuna had promised her.

What if her fourteen-year-old daughter, Indu, was listening from somewhere inside?

'Why the recipe? Are you having a party?'

'Oh no. My husband's away. He took the first flight to Bombay this morning.'

He was being cautious too.

'Oh, he'd promised to give me a new video tape.'

'You can look for it here on your way back from the office. I don't know which one it is.'

'I may. Around seven.'

If he came in the evening for the video or a book, she would offer him a drink as a matter of courtesy. By the time they got to the second drink it would be late. The children would greet him and go off to the study. She would tell them to have dinner and join him for the third drink. They were on the brink of some happening. That day, she had given Indu and Sunny permission to go for an evening show of a film, pretending that they had insisted on going. The maidservant had gone to find out about her mother's illness and would return only the following day. 'I'll show you a film when the children are not around, 'Strictly for adults.' It had been a promise. They had a clear three hours, all the loopholes had been closed. What attractive quality had his grey eyes seen in her that Yamuna, who was so much younger, did not possess? It was then that the long-distance telephone call had come unexpectedly from her village.

The cowdung used to plaster the sun-drenched courtyard had begun to flake off. The waves of heat rising from it flowed into the verandah. Cursing everyone because she was so upset, Vishalam got up and said: 'I've got a bad headache, Seetha, I'm going to lie down.'

Seethalakshmi said to herself: 'The two of us came together, my husband and I. This headache! I've heard that some people who use hair dye have a perpetual headache.'

The sick man swallowed four or five spoons of kanji at night. The doctor came again at nine o'clock and examined him. He decided there was no need for an injection. Vishalam opened her purse as he was leaving but Seethalakshmi had already given him fifteen rupees by then.

'I would have given it,' said Vishalam.

'What does it matter who gives it?'

Kutti Narayanan asked all of them to go to bed. 'I'm not going to sleep. I'll call you if it's necessary.'

He sat down in the sick man's room, reading the *Ramayanam* in a soft voice.

Achu asked the cheruman, Thami, to sleep on the verandah so that he could run up to his house with a message if there was any change and made ready to leave.

'Do you want me to send any mattresses?'

Seethalakshmi said, 'No.'

Narayani Amma spread out a mat near the bed and lay down. Vishalam tried to persuade her to sleep in comfort in one of the other rooms.

Kutti Narayanan opened the *Ramayanam* at random at the Sundara Kandam. It was tough to read and he stopped after a while. He leaned against the wall and closed his eyes. If he felt sleepy, he thought, he would make some black tea. Later.

Vishalam could not sleep. There were no mosquitoes but she still felt suffocated because there was no fan. A month of planning, of exchanging glances and meaningful telephone calls—and then, when the opportunity arrived, everything had gone wrong. When would it happen again? If she hadn't had the car, she could have asked him to escort her home as soon as the long distance call came. But when she had the car and the driver, what would people think if she arrived with her husband's assistant? She should have mixed some gin and cordial and packed it into her briefcase. These people would never recognize the smell. At least it would have made it easier for her to fall asleep.

'Are you asleep, Edathi?'

'H'm...'

Seethalakshmi said, spreading her mat on the floor, 'I'll sleep here.'

'No, sleep on the other side.' Seethalakshmi made her bed, pretending she had not heard.

Vishalam placed her elbow over her eyes and shut her eyes tight. Her husband would have to go on many more official tours. The problem was to clear all the obstacles in their way—Yamuna, the children, the servant maid.

Seethalakshmi turned the light off. Vishalam felt the darkness was a relief. She thought she had a strip of Calmpose tablets in her handbag, but could not find it. Should she look once again, she wondered. She decided not to.

'Are you looking for a suitable match for Indu?'

'In two or three years. She's studying, after all.'

Indu was only seventeen. Maybe Seetha wanted Indu to be married off so that she could watch her older sister become a grandmother. Seetha asked her something else but she didn't answer. Let her think I'm trying to sleep, thought Vishalam.

Seethalakshmi tossed from side to side on her mat, unable to sleep. Were there things crawling over it? The mat had been rolled up and kept in the room used to store paddy. With her father in this condition, Seethalakshmi did not want to sleep in her husband's room lest it upset her sister. That's why she had found a mat and spread it here

'I wonder what these things are that are biting me,' said Seethalakshmi, sitting up and scratching her neck and back.

She got up, went out, gently closing the door behind her and made her way to Padmanabhan's room. She saw that Kutti Narayanan was dozing, leaning against the wall, and her aunt was asleep.

Seethalakshmi sat down on the bed and Padmanabhan moved nearer the wall to make room for her.

'Are you asleep?'

He grunted, 'H'm...'

All his problems would be solved if he was given charge of the project. He would certainly have to appoint some people on the strength of recommendations from the ministers. But he could take money from all the others. The Brahmin, Dharmalingam, would manage it efficiently if he were given a small share. And if enquiries were ever made at a later date, he could always plead ignorance. He had never demanded anything from anyone, he would say. No one who had got into the Company would dare make a complaint until he was confirmed. By that time, he would have gone back.

He would wait until the next evening. After that, if this situation continued, Seetha could stay back. He would leave for Palghat by the State Transport bus in the evening. If news of the death came to him while the M.D. was still in the office, he could go straight to his room and inform him. He had to do that. He had to tell the M.D. he could not stay any longer and that he would undertake any duties the M.D. was pleased to entrust him with. Then he would walk out with a sad face. It would be a moment replete with drama. News of a death would perhaps benefit him more than a gift of Black Label whisky. He moved Seethalakshmi's hand which was lying on his chest and tried to get some sleep.

Kutti Narayanan got up as the crows began to caw. He wiped off the spittle that had oozed from the patient's lips and called him softly: 'Master, would you like something to drink?'

A low grunt, like a reply. Kutti Narayanan went out and performed his ablutions, first below the palm tree at the boundary of the compound and then at the well. Then he boiled some water and made black coffee for himself. He mixed some Horlicks for the sick man. Well, there were plenty of women around. Let them make breakfast, he thought. He parted the patient's lips and poured in two teaspoonfuls of Horlicks.

Narayani Amma sat up.

'See if you can get him to swallow four teaspoonsful,' he said to her, then opened the front door and went out into the courtyard. It was the time when the days were growing shorter. The sun would not rise till later. He woke up the cheruman, Thami, and asked him to fetch the milk. They would probably not make anything for breakfast. It would be just as well to send for some food from the other house.

Achu came in, flashing a five-battery torch. He had a boy with him.

'Nothing special …?'

'No.'

'I got up when Raju arrived. Didn't sleep after that.'

'This is Bhaskaran's …'

'… second son.'

Kutti Narayanan smiled at Raju.

'I must have seen you as a small boy. Isn't your father coming?'

'He said to find out the news and telephone him.'

'Go in and see him.'

As soon as Raju went in, Achu said, 'Today's another busy day. I have to meet the M.P. when he comes to the Travellers' Bungalow. Then go to the Executive Engineer's office. What can I do?'

Kutti Naryanan consoled him. 'Go along. Nothing will happen in the daytime. Don't expect anything until after nightfall.'

When day had broken and the sick man's room became bright, Kutti Naryanan went up to him and gave him a close look. Was there a change in the rhythm of the breathing? He said to Seethalakshmi, who came in sleepily, 'There's a slight change.'

Padmanabhan came in as he was explaining the change in the rhythm of breathing that only he could detect. Seethalakshmi looked at Padmanabhan straight in the eye and said, 'Kutti Narayanan says there's a change.'

Padmanabhan looked at Kutti Narayanan questioningly and he nodded in assent.

'There'll be a complete change after sunset, that's what today will be like.'

Vishalam came in by then. It gave Seethalakshmi an inner satisfacion to see Vishalam looking dishevelled. Now she really looked older than her. Look at the dark circles under her eyes, thought Seethalakshmi. And the wrinkles on her face. It was the husbands who let their wives spend half their salary on cosmetics who were to be blamed.

Vishalam asked Raju: 'Won't your father come?'

'He asked me to find out how he is and telephone.'

Seethalakshmi suddenly realised she had not paid Raju any attention. She smiled and placed her hand on his shoulder. 'Did you come by bus or by train?' she asked.

'By train. Then I caught the last bus from Kuttippuram.'

Achu came to the door and asked the women: 'Shouldn't we get the doctor again?'

No one replied directly. Narayani Amma said to Kutti

Narayanan, 'He finds it hard to pass urine. If that were corrected, it would be a great relief to him.'

Kutti Narayanan found a reason: 'He has to drink some fluid first.'

'Let the doctor come and see him, Achu, for our satisfaction.' She massaged the sick man's hand gently. 'All we want, my Lord Guruvayoorappa, is that he shouldn't linger long and suffer.'

'Mother, go home if you like. You can come back later.' His mother did not reply. When Padmanabhan came in, Achu said: 'I'm going out. There's been a boundary dispute and the Circle Inspector is expected. Then our M.P. is coming this way. He'll be upset if he doesn't see me.'

'Achu, if you're going home, tell them to send the refreshments if they're ready.'

Achu cut Kutti Narayanan short and said angrily: 'Look Nair, tea, snacks, meals: they'll all be here on time. All we need is for you to stay with Uncle. The women will see to the kitchen.'

Kutti Narayanan no longer dared to ask about the Panchayat President's daughter's engagement after hearing this outburst. Which side of the bed had the man got up on, he wondered.

By the time the women finished their baths, one by one, and came out, a huge vessel filled with three layers of food had arrived from the ancestral house.

The patient swallowed six teaspoonsful of kanji at noon. But he did not open his eyes.

'He's swallowing fluids all right,' said Padmanabhan, sounding surprised. Kutti Narayanan grunted, then whispered: 'But his breathing. Did you see the way he's breathing?'

Padmanabhan led Kutti Narayanan out of the room.

'What if I leave at five? Sita can stay behind.'

Kutti Narayanan pondered. 'No, if you ask my opinion, I think it will all be over tonight. You can leave tomorrow at midday after everything is finished.'

'I have hundereds of things to attend to there, Kutti Narayanan Nair.'

'Be patient for one more night.'

When Padmanabhan left, Raju came up to him, smiling. He had Bhaskaran's big, broad teeth.

'Isn't it enough to join in the seventh-day ceremonies?'

'Yes, that's enough.'

'Someone said if you're at the cremation, you have to stay until the fourteenth day.'

'No, that's not necessary.'

'I have to go on an excursion the day after tomorrow, at night.'

'So you have to reach Coimbatore the day after. You can easily do that.'

There were some visitors who came to see the sick man. Dignitaries from the village. They stood at his door for a while.

'The President's not here?' asked Kutti Narayanan by way of greeting.

'He'll come.'

Nambiar, the farmer with a tractor, poked Kutti Narayanan playfully in his stomach.

'No exercise and endless eating—that's why you have this potbelly!'

They sat in the portico and asked Padmanabhan about the daily wage rate in Palghat. They argued about the reasons for the wages having risen to seventeen rupees in Kizhakkemuri.

As they were about to leave, Kutti Narayanan put in an appearance again as the representative of the household.

'It would be good if this weather holds and it doesn't rain, isn't that so, Kutti Narayana?'

At dusk, the sound of the drums from the Shiva temple in the distance wafted in with the western wind that blew down the slope of the hill. The Thiruvegappura drummers. Was it Achu or Raman? If it was Raman, there would be some fun at the finish. It was not for nothing he had attached himself to Raman at the temple festival last year.

Seethalakshmi lit the oil lamp at dusk. Narayani Amma began to chant her prayers loudly. Kutti Narayanan washed his

hands and legs, smeared vibhuti over his forehead, sat down by
the lamp and opened the *Ramayanam.*

It was a good augury, the book fell open at the page where
the salvation of the bird, Jatayu, was described. He read two
lines, closed his eyes, said a prayer. Then he opened his eyes and
looked around him. Only Narayani Amma was there. He looked
closely at her to find out whether she had grasped the
significance of what he had read. Narayani Amma sat there,
massaging her legs, swaying to and fro, her eyes shut.

Kutti Narayanan went in and checked the patient's
breathing. He was very restless. Maybe this was a sign that the
last breath would soon be drawn. Was there any Ganga water
in the house, he wondered.

The sick man groaned. A blue jay cried out from a tree in
the yard. He saw Narayani Amma's look reaching out towards
him from behind her thick glasses. She understood that
language. And so did he.

Kutti Narayanan went up to Master and stroked his
forehead. He massaged his limbs.

The sick man was struggling to say something.

'What do you want? What is it? What?'

Narayani Amma came up to him too. Master's words could
barely be made out through his groans.

'I want to get up.'

Narayani Amma shouted excitedly: 'Achu! Rajasekharan!'

Everyone came running into the room.

'Let's make him sit up,' said Kutti Narayanan.

'Should we?'

'We must.'

Together, the men lifted Master and propped him up against
the wall on his pillow.

'Water ...' groaned Master.

A steel glass containing Horlicks was brought to his lips.
Kutti Narayan noticed Master's hands going slowly up towards
the glass.

Master opened his eyes slowly, moaning all the time. They

were all there before him. Seethalakshmi, who had been standing behind Rajasekharan, came forward.

'Father, Father … it's I …'

Master's tired eyes looked around, focusing on no one in particular.

Master moved the glass away from his lips.

Kutti Narayanan said, 'I am Kutti Narayanan.'

Master muttered, between groans: 'It's not hot, heat it up.'

Kutti Narayanan thought to himself, as he walked to the kitchen, he'll never give up his obstinacy. He felt confused. This was a strange kind of change. Maybe it was possible—a stage just preceding death when everything altered. Maybe there were only moments left now for the end. The senior most member of the Poothottil family, the village headman's father and Kalathil Kurup: Kutti Narayanan recalled the same thing having taken place in all three cases.

The next morning, the children stood around the sick man who was seated with his back resting against the wall.

Vishalam said, 'If there's anything you need, Father, just ask Achu Ettan to call me.'

The old man did not say anything.

'I'll drop Seetha at the junction before I go.'

Master nodded slowly.

Seetha touched her father's forehead. 'We can go when you're recovered. We'll have the eye surgery done there.'

Vishalam hesitated for a while, then said, 'I am leaving, Father.'

Master nodded.

Kutti Narayanan accompanied the women on their way out.

His hope that they would give him something was futile. Murmuring something to each other, they stepped into the courtyard, ignoring him completely even though he followed them like a shadow.

When he came back, Raju was standing at the door of the room, looking confused.

'I'm going. Please tell Grandfather, Kutti Narayanan.'

'Go up to him, child, and tell him.'

Raju went up to the bed. Master saw him stand there hesitantly and asked, 'Time to go?'

'H'm...'

'Get going then.'

Relieved, Raju left. Kutti Narayanan waited uncertainly. Then he said to Narayani Amma, 'I'm going out. I'll be back.'

He went out without waiting for a reply, his mind seething with anger at all the people who had united to deceive him.

Master gazed at Narayani Amma who was seated on the floor with her legs stretched out.

'Don't you want to go?'

Narayani Amma grunted in reply.

'Where's Achu?'

'He's gone out. He'll be back.'

Master cleared the phlegm in his throat and said softly: 'Are you listening? If I fall seriously ill again, don't send for the children. They've hundreds of things to do. No telegrams, no phone calls. Don't inform them till you're sure it's all over.'

His words trailed off as he gasped for breath.

Master looked at a distant point outside the window and murmured: 'Let whoever is free come after that. Tell Achu as well.'

Narayani Amma looked at her brother. The eyes dulled with age that gazed out through the window were filled with tears.

'You're crying, Ettan!'

'No, of course not ... My head feels hot, that's why my eyes are watering ...'

Master rubbed his eyes. 'You can go too.'

His sister did not answer. She kept chanting in her mind: 'Narayana! Narayana!'

Kadugannawa: A Travel Note

He had been twenty-two when he wandered through the Himalayan foothills with a shoulder bag that contained two sets of clothes and a camera. He had ridden a horse over a narrow path that went from Ijat Nagar to Almora. He had drunk bhang mixed with milk, gone to sleep and woken up to find himself lying on a boulder overlooking a chasm. That was long ago. Now, he avoided journeys. He seldom spent a night in a strange place. Even if he climbed a few steps, it took him three or four minutes to recover his breath. It was a nuisance carrying around pills for his blood pressure and tubes of insulin for injections. Nevertheless, he accepted the invitation to visit Sri Lanka. Although he did not have anything significant to say about the role newspapers could play in the development of Southeast Asia. He agreed because the invitation was from Sri Lanka. There was a place there that he had always wanted to see. Kadugannawa.

His colleagues at the Madras office had told him that he needed to be at the airport only two hours before departure. No one observed the rule that passengers to foreign countries had to report three hours in advance. But he got there very early. There was a time when he used to arrive only after everyone had checked in and his name was being announced and had run up the ladder just before it was removed. Now, if he did anything in a hurry, the thudding of his heart would grow very loud.

The departure lounge was almost empty. The plane would

leave on time. A group of Sri Lankans suddenly trooped in with bags and bundles and the lounge was full.

When taking class for new recruits to journalism, they always said, keep your eyes and ears open. A story worth reporting could happen any minute somewhere around you.

Were these people refugees? They couldn't be, refugees were being sent back by sea. These people were carrying back not only mixers and grinders, but even fresh vegetables from Madras. Maybe he could strike up a conversation with a couple of them—about comparative prices, or their new President. He could even ask them for their reaction—albeit delayed—to the news of the assassination of our former Prime Minister. No, he was not going to write a report of any kind.

There were women among the Sri Lankans. He suddenly thought of his mother. She used to call them Shingalathis. Sri Lanka was the land of the Shingalas and Shingalathis.

The last to join them were two *bhikshus*, Buddhist monks. He looked at them attentively when they sat down on two seats near him—one was a woman, a *bhikshuni*.

He had planned to make this trip in 1981. Pereira, a journalist friend from Goa who worked with *The Ceylon Observer*, had offered to make arrangements to take him wherever he wanted to go. He had even been ready to write an article on "An Investigation made by an Indian Journalist." But three days before he was due to leave, a rebellion broke out in Sri Lanka and a state of emergency was declared. Pereira called and asked him to postpone his journey. He agreed—the country was nearby after all, he could go there any time he wanted. But it was a mistake to have delayed the trip so long.

They announced that boarding had started on the plane to Sri Lanka. The tourists rushed to the gate, not bothering to form a queue. Even the saffron-clad bhikshuni forced her way forward like the rest.

A young man standing beside him laughed and said: 'Look at that!'

He laughed too.

'To Calambo?'

'Yes.'

'What's the climate like there?'

Which climate did he mean? The insurgency or the weather?

'I don't know.'

He made a note mentally: you did not say "Colombo", it was "Calambo".

Although he had a window seat, his view was blocked by the wing of the plane. It did not matter. He was not going to write a travelogue. He had sometimes written about countries he had visited in order to justify trips that were supposed to be on duty. He had often started them with the first thing he saw as the plane landed.

He glanced at his watch. Just as he calculated that it would take ten more minutes to land, the first announcement was made. He hurriedly filled up the immigration form and opened his briefcase again. The passport, the ticket, the letters and fax messages from the organisers of the seminar, were all there. Needless anxieties and fears filled one's mind as one grew older. Otherwise, why did he always check that the door had been bolted at night even after his daughter had told him that she had bolted it?

Dr Ramachandran had said: 'Mr Venugopalan, people get like that when they grow old.'

Air India had once made a mistake about the date and there had been no one to receive him when he walked out at Tokyo airport. He had gone by taxi to the Asia Centre. In a few hours he had knocked on the door of the friend and his astonished wife, who had been expecting him only the next day. The spirit of adventure had been his constant companion in those days.

Wouldn't the organisers of the seminar be waiting for him? He began to feel anxious.

While waiting for his baggage, he remembered: hadn't a bomb exploded here once, killing a number of people? When had it been? President Premadasa had died a few months ago. In a bomb blast in the middle of the city. He thought of how the Buddha had come to this island, which had been ruled by asuras and demons who had slaughtered and murdered.

When a bloodthirsty gang surrounded him, the Buddha smiled. Violent winds blew and lightning flashed. The demons trembled in fear.

'Give me a place where I can sit down,' said the Buddha.

'Deliver us from fear and we will give you this whole island.'

'You will no longer experience fear.'

He rebuked himself: do not be afraid. Life is only an interlude after one has made a treaty with death. He thought of the game of chess in Bergman's "Seventh Seal". He read about Vedanta and Buddhism nowadays in order to achieve freedom from fear.

One had to understand that danger lurked here all the time. Maybe that was why the Chief Editor, who never refused an invitation from abroad, had chosen him to take part in this seminar. He had not told the Chief Editor about the secret of Kadugannawa.

What a relief! A young man was waiting for him, holding a placard with his name on it. He went up to him, dragging his suitcase.

'I am P.K. Venugopal.' The young man took charge of his suitcase. They walked out.

At last he had come to the country he had thought he would never visit. Although late, Sri Lanka had invited him.

As the taxi sped forward, he looked at the kiosks and the small workshops on the roadside and thought they look like the shops in Changaramkulam, at home. He had not realised the airport was so far from the city. It took thirty-five minutes. As he signed the hotel register:

'Welcome, Mr Venugopal! I am Ashley Gunatilake.'

They had talked over the telephone twice. He had round, protuberant eyes, and the hint of a small beard that looked as if it had been left by mistake on his chin. He thought the man resembled some old black singer whose name he could not remember. He seemed to be bathed in sweat beneath his black suit.

He could see a bit of the sea from the fourth-floor room. There was a building opposite with a flag flying on top. He looked at the helicopter circling above it. Gunatilake said, 'Security—that's the President's office.'

Gunatilake parted the window curtains. 'Look, there are naval boats on guard in front.'

He told Gunatilake that it was his first visit to Sri Lanka. He had wanted to come earlier but had not been able to. He thought he would not mention the old connections now.

'It's been a very busy day, so I couldn't come to the airport.'

'That's all right. After all, you're here now, Mr Gunatilake.'

'Call me Ashley. Let's have a drink.'

He took out two cans of beer from the small refrigerator. Venugopalan declined.

'Orange juice? Coke?'

No, he didn't want anything. He did not want to tell Gunatilake that he had to take forty units of insulin a day.

'With your permission.' Ashley gulped down his first beer straight from the can in a minute. He opened the second one, poured the contents into a glass and lit a cigarette.

'That's a relief. What a day!'

'What's the situation like now? Are things calm?'

'It's always calm. But danger can strike any moment. Do you see that roof that looks like a steeple? The bomb that killed Premadasa exploded beneath it.' What Kennedy said was right: "If someone wants to kill me, no security network can prevent it. All it needs is that one man be ready to give up his life to take mine!"

Ashley Gunatilake was an official in the Ministry of Information. He could not be more than thirty-five. Venugopalan felt that his tone held the maturity of an elder statesman.

'The LTTE recruits twelve-year-old children now. After the massacre in the military camp, fifteen-year-old teenagers queue up every day in our recruiting offices, eager to take revenge. Have you heard what Shelley said?'

'Who?'

'Shelley. P.B. Shelley, the English poet. "War is an

entertainment for rulers, a blessing for priests, a matter of logic for practitioners of law, a trade for mercenaries.'''

In the space of five minutes, the man had quoted Kennedy and Shelley. He must thank his stars that he had Ashley as his host.

'Mr Ashley, I wrote that I wanted to visit certain places ...'

'After the seminar tomorrow, we've set apart Saturday and Sunday for sight-seeing. There's so much to see in this country. There'll be a person from the Department of Tourism with you.'

'Please, Mr Ashley. Come with me.'

'Let's see. I never tire of looking at historical monuments. Let's see. Any particular places you want to see?'

'Kandy.'

'Everyone goes there. The fourteenth-century capital. Three hours from here. What else?'

He said hesitantly, 'I think it's somewhere near there. Kadugannawa.'

'Oh, Kadugannawa? I know the place, it's on our way.'

Ashley's father-in-law was from there. He had moved to Colombo about ten years ago.

'He is now ...'

'He died last December.'

He thought Gunatilake would ask, what importance could Kadugannawa have for an elderly journalist from Kerala? He had decided to say that relatives of his used to live there.

Ashley looked at his watch and got up.

'The seminar is at five tomorrow. It will do if you're ready by four.' He held out his visiting card. 'Have a good rest.'

He placed the empty beer cans on top of the refrigerator and left.

A little later, Venugopalan went down to the hotel lobby. He browsed through the books and stationery in the shops. Compared to India, the prices were higher.

He stood outside the hotel for a while. The lights on the long road along the seashore came on suddenly. There was a military checkpost right in front. He went back to his room, called room service and ordered his meal for seven. Then he changed into a checked lungi and relaxed on the sofa.

What had it looked like, the face of the little girl seated on a steel trunk, twirling a bunch of keys? The face of the little Shingalathi girl? There had been two calendars at home at the time. Did one have a picture of baby Saroja? Or of Ashwathamma? Someone in the movies, anyway. The other one had Sri Krishna. Whenever he opened Amma's four-legged wooden box to examine its contents, Sri Krishna's reddish eyes used to stare accusingly at him. He was certain that the girl from Ceylon had a prettier face than the movie actress. She had a squarish face and shoulder-length hair. He had only a hazy picture of her in his mind now.

Venugopalan had gone to Devi Oppu's house only after he had decided on this trip. Devi Oppu was his father's niece. He had gone there to tell her that he would not be able to attend her youngest daughter's wedding.

'Once this is over, I'll be relieved. It was just our good fortune that this proposal came through,' said Devi Oppu.

He told her he was not sure he could attend the wedding. 'The children will come. I'll be in Ceylon at that time.'

Devi Oppu was upset.

'It's office work—a journalists' conference. And then, since it's in Ceylon …'

'Haven't you been to Ceylon, Venu?'

'No. I planned to go a number of times but never made it.'

Devi Oppu remembered that Venu's older brothers, Kuttettan and Rajettan, had lived in Ceylon when they were children. His mother had returned to India before Appu was born.

Some of their relatives dropped by to ask about the wedding arrangements.

'Ah, Venu, it's quite a while since we saw you.'

Devi Oppu said to them: 'Venu is going to Ceylon, so he can't come for the wedding. He can visit the place Uncle worked in, can't you, Venu?'

He smiled. 'Maybe. I'll try.'

'What was the name of the place where Uncle worked? I can't remember ...'

'Kadugannawa.'

He would never forget the name. His older brothers used to write the address on the letters Amma wrote and he used to be the one who posted them.

Their neighbour, Visalakshi Amma, asked: 'Didn't a child come from there once, Devi?'

Devi Oppu said, 'Who knows whether they are still alive! It was such a long time ago. Her name was Leela.'

Venugopalan had made calculations earlier. The Shingalathi who was said to have lived with his father was not likely to be alive now. If she was, she would be at least ninety.

'Leela was my age. She might be alive.'

Venugopalan was astonished. He used to speak about her often, it was an intriguing story. A mother with four sons. She wanted a daughter very much. Then her husband came home from abroad after many years and there was a little girl with him. A rumour arose that she was his daughter and there was a violent quarrel in the house.

For some reason, Venugopalan had thought the child was younger than him.

'Devi Oppu, wasn't she ... wasn't that girl younger than me?'

'Oh no! You were nine then. She had her first period when we were playing in the yard of Marathattu. I remember it very well.'

He had heard the story of what happened when the girl went with Father to his ancestral house. For two whole days she had sat next to the wooden grain chest in the southern room. She did not even have a bath or go to the toilet. Devi Oppu and her mother had tried their best, then they had gone to Father very hesitantly and told him about her. It was only after that that the girl began going out to play with the other children.

'She must have been twelve or thirteen at the time, I'm sure of that. She had a very well-developed body.'

He had not known that the girl from Ceylon had had her

first period then. Venugopalan calculated. She must be sixty-two or sixty-three now.

He remembered the celebration the night Father came home. Two chickens were killed in the northern yard. His older brother had played records on the gramophone that Father had brought. Father had entertained their uncles and the village bigwigs in a room upstairs. They heard the Tamil songs played there late into the night. At some time during the night, after the guests left, Mother and Father had had a quarrel. He had woken up from sleep with a start hearing his mother talk loudly. The uncle who had come with Father had spoken of the Shingalathi.

Father left the next morning for Vanneri, his own village, taking the child with him. They stayed there three months and then left for Ceylon.

None of Father's children went to Vanneri, though all of them, especially the youngest, Venugopalan, liked going there. They always served tasty snacks for evening tea in Father's place. Their speciality was a pancake made with powdered country dates and rayi grass. Ammu Oppu, who presided over the kitchen, knew a secret recipe for making sweet payasam with mathok flour. She often gave the children roasted ayini seeds.

But Mother would tell everyone: 'Stay here and eat what you get. You needn't go anywhere.'

The waiter removed the dinner dishes. Venugopalan stood at the window, looking out. He could still hear the helicopter. The gunboats were not visible now. Now and then, he saw the fiery eye of a lighted cigarette in the booth on the roadside where soldiers stood guard.

The traffic had almost stopped but the town was still not asleep. He parted the curtains to let in the light of dawn and went to bed.

He called Ashley in the morning. No one picked up the phone. He got through at the third attempt.

'Did you sleep well?'

'Yes, very well.'

Did the paper for the seminar have to be distributed in

advance? No. The man from Bangladesh had not arrived. Patel from Bombay had come …

'Ashley, the sight-seeing trip?'

'Don't worry, I'll arrange it. The car will come at four. Be ready.'

It was possible that some of the Malayalees still left in the country would come for the seminar conducted by the journalists of the SAARC if they knew that a P.K. Venugopalan Nair was one of the speakers. If any of the older people remembered Father …

His older brother had said that Father had had a certain standing among the Ceylon Malayalees. He had seen the photograph taken at a reception given to the High Commissioner in Ceylon, who was a Malayalee, in Father's suitcase. He had been sure that Father was among those who stood in the back row.

His other brother, Rajettan, had been, as usual, sceptical. But the older brother had argued: "Isn't Father's address proof enough that he was well-known—K.M. Nair, Kadugannawa, Ceylon."

He had a faint hope that he would meet some elderly Malayalees at the seminar.

When he arrived at the seminar hall with the paper he had written laboriously over three days, there were only about fifteen people there. He waited outside. No, there was no one who had come because he had seen a Malayalee's name on the list.

There were six people on the dais. Venugopalan pretended to listen with interest to the Sri Lankan official who inaugurated the conference with a speech on the conflict between established powers and newly-awakened ones.

The conference was over sooner than he had expected.

Ashley had been in the audience. He said they could start at eight the next morning. They would spend the night at Anuradhapura. They would travel as the guests of the Department of Tourism, in a car they would provide.

'Ashley, you must come with me.'

'I'll try.'

'Don't say that, you must come.'

It may have been because he had communicated with Ashley through phone calls and letters that he looked upon him now as a close friend.

It rained at night but the morning sky was clear and bright.

Ashley arrived at eight thirty in a car from the Department of Tourism.

As they drove along, he asked Ashley about his family. He had two daughters and his wife worked in a bank. He had been educated in London and had worked there for two years in the Ceylon High Commission.

Ashley knew the history and legends of Ceylon and remembered dates accurately. As they walked around, looking at the historic monuments, Ashley described the age of Devanampriya Tissa. The first Buddha Vihara, Mihinthale. It was Emperor Asoka's son, Mahendra, who came here with the message of the Buddha. Mihinthale was named after Mahendra. Asoka's daughter, Sanghamitra, brought a branch of the bodhi tree and planted it there. 'Take it down if you want to—Sanghamitra, third century B.C. The wall around it was put up by Vikramaraja Simha …'

He made some notes to satisfy Ashley.

There was a military camp outside the boundary wall. Once, a tourist bus that seemed to be carrying pilgrims had pulled up at the spot. The passengers had got down and pulled out AK-47s from beneath their saffron robes. They were Tamil militants. Sixty-seven people had died in the shooting that followed. There had been devotees and vendors who sold flowers at the roadside among the dead. It was after that that the military camp had been set up to guard the place.

Ashley bought a flower-tray from the mandapam in front of the bodhi tray, placed five white flowers on it and prayed for a minute.

'Ashley, you're …'

'I'm a Buddhist.'

During the British rule, many people had taken Christian names in order to get admission in schools. The names continued to be used through generations. Ashley's grandfather was also an Ashley.

Ashley said, as they were looking at the shrine of the Buddha in samadhi and the Copper Palace:

'The king who embraced the religion of the Buddha disbanded the army. The soldiers dug wells and ponds and began to cultivate the land. Two men who came from Tamil Nadu to sell horses saw this country without an army and made their plans. They went back, returned with six boatloads of soldiers and captured the land. That is the story of the first invasion.'

'You are the people who always looked out for opportunities to invade,' said Ashley, smiling.

Venugopalan was feeling tired, walking around the ruins of the old viharas.

They had arranged to spend the night at the rest house on the banks of the Nuwara Mewa lake.

Ashley took out a bottle of "Old Arrack" and said, 'I prefer this to foreign whisky.'

Venugopalan mentioned his ailments and declined a drink. It had grown dark outside.

'It is new moon tomorrow.'

Venugopalan was anxious to know what the next day's programme was.

'You remember what I told you, Ashley?'

'Oh, yes. Kadugannawa. We're going that way. It's a pleasant place. The view from the top is beautiful. But there's nothing else there.'

Venugopalan said hesitantly: 'My father worked there for some time. And some other people from my village. An uncle ...'

'That's incredible! We'll go there.'

Venugopalan pretended to listen to the stories Ashley was telling with interest, while he remembered that it was after he finished college that his father had returned home for good. Their relatives and the villagers presumed that he would bring home plenty of money after having worked in Ceylon for thirty-one years. Venugopalan's mother had died by then. Father had come twice while she was still alive. He would come home in the morning and go back to Vanneri in the evening. Amma would arrange for two extra vegetable preparations and scrambled eggs to be made, but would not appear before him. When it was time to eat, she would ask one of the children to tell him that the leaves had been laid. Meenakshi Edathi, who helped Amma in the kitchen, would serve the food.

Devi Oppu's brother who was Father's eldest nephew made discreet enquiries about Father's savings and told them the money had been deposited in a bank.

The important people in the village came visiting every evening. Brandy bottles brought from Ceylon were opened and Vijayettan sent scrambled eggs and fried pappadams upstairs. When the bottles from Ceylon were finished, Vijayettan got some more from Thrissur. At the end of ten days, Father placed bottles of arrack distilled by Unneeri before his guests and said:

'You know our Unneeri. No foreign liquor can be compared to the liquor he distils.' His guests nodded agreement. From the next evening, Father found himself alone.

When the "Old Arrack" bottle was half empty, Ashley got up. Sweat was running down his forehead. He wanted to speak about a romantic interlude in his life in London, but postponed it to the next day.

Ashley was silent while they ate in the dining hall. He stumbled while they went back upstairs and laughed when Venugopalan put out his hand to steady him.

'Never mind. The Old Arrack's giving me a good kick!'

Venugopalan had to help him open the door of his room.

'Goodnight.'

'Goodnight.'

Once alone in his own room, Venugopalan took off his shoes. His feet felt free. It was clear that he was no longer fit for long journeys.

Vijayettan, who read detective novels day and night, seemed to have taken on the role of a detective himself, with the blessings of the womenfolk. He would waylay the postman before he reached the house and take away the letters addressed to Father. He would take them to the kitchen, steam them open, read them and then reseal them and hand them over to Father. However, he did not gather any fresh information. Father always kept his keys with him. Vijayettan found some old keys and managed to open Father's trunk after many attempts. He did not find any documents or old records. There was only an old Kozhikode Imperial Bank passbook, cancelled after transactions had been discontinued. He did not even get hold of Madhava Ammama's address.

When Vijayettan died, Venugopalan was working in the Delhi office of the newspaper. On his next visit home, he went to see his father's sisters in Vanneri. They told him old stories about Vijayettan and wept. Then they recounted his exploits as a detective and laughed.

'Venu, do you know why Father did not bring anything back with him?'

Father had had financial difficulties from the moment he came back. He began to borrow money from the man to whom they sold the yield from the coconut trees. His younger brother, who had looked after the household till then, said: 'My elder brother is here now. He can look after things,' and moved to his wife's house, some distance away. He lived on the income he made from the property there.

After many years, Vijayettan seemed to have found out the truth somehow. Father had owned a rubber estate when he came away. He had given it to the daughter he had by the Shingalathi and arranged a marriage for her before he returned.

This was news to Venugopalan. 'How did he find that out?'

'Vijayettan wrote to several people in Ceylon. He must have got the information through them.'

Father's younger sister said: 'Let her live in comfort. Whether she's one of us or not, she's a woman, isn't she?' Venu was distressed. Even when he earned a salary of three hundred rupees, he used to send a hundred to Father. Father used to tell everyone he met that his sons were not looking after him properly. There was the rubber estate he had gifted. And money as well, Venu did not know how much. Distress turned into anger.

The next morning, Ashley knocked on his door, dressed in jeans and a bright red T-shirt.

'Ready, Mr Venu?'

He was not yet ready.

They went to Polaneruwa. To the Parakrama Sagar lake that King Parakrama Bahu had made. Then there was Nishangamallan, who had woken up his workers in the middle of the night and made them chisel accounts of his great and noble deeds on stone.

'When will we reach Kadugannawa?'

'Our next stop in Kandy. We'll have lunch there. Kadugannawa is nearby. Don't you want to see Sigiriya?'

He did not show much interest. Ashley told him the story of the fifth century king, Dasasena, who had fought the Tamil invaders eighteen times. His nephew and the son he had had by his concubine joined forces and took him prisoner. The son he had had by his queen ran away to India. Kashyapan, who had taken the king prisoner, was upset when he found no gold or jewels in the palace. He asked his father: 'Where is all the wealth?'

Venugopalan was suddenly interested in Dasasena's story. All through the ages, there had been children who became furious when they could not find the wealth their fathers had amassed.

'And then?'

'The king said he would show him where the wealth was if he was taken to the large lake he had made. He was taken there in a chariot. The king stepped into the lake eagerly and drank water. He swam around for a while. Then, splashing in the water, he said: 'Here, this is my treasure!' The story goes that Kashyapan buried the king alive in a stone chamber.

Venugopalan decided to visit Sigiriya. It was an isolated, rocky hill in the middle of a forest. All around it lay the ruins of ramparts and trenches. Afraid of the Crown Prince who had gone away to India, Kashyapan built a palace on top of the hill. There was only one entrance—through the mouth of a lion carved in stone. Only one person could pass at a time through it. And so he ruled, from the top of the hill.

'Mogallanan, the Crown Prince, came back with an army and challenged Kashyapan, who came downhill to fight him. When he was defeated, Kashyapan plunged a sword into his neck and killed himself.'

Venugopalan stood before the steps leading into the lion's mouth. The left foreleg of the gigantic sculpture of the lion still stood, and three claws. Ashley stood between them and said, 'Look, the claw comes up to my knee. You can guess how huge the lion was!'

On the sides of the steps that led to the top were the figures of ten beautiful women. On the opposite side, on a wall polished like a mirror were graffiti scrawled by visitors.

'Come!'

Venugopalan climbed up with difficulty.

Ashley read out some of the things people had written. 'Saw the Lion King below. Do not want to see the palace of the King on top.'

Ashley stood there for a long time, reading and enjoying the words.

'Look, this is a ninth century line. He must have been a poet. "I found here the sky of my dreams."' Mogallanan's army must have lined up below, the place where rocks were strewn around.

'What were Kashyapan's soldiers doing while they climbed nearer?'

Ashley explained that the army had reached there on the night of the new moon.

We reached Kandy at noon. Ashley prayed with five white flowers at the great temple where the Buddha's tooth was kept.

Pointing to the gardens beside the lake and the Queens' bath-houses, Ashley said, 'Lawrence came here. D.H. Lawrence. In 1922.'

Lawrence had been angry with the dancers who performed before the Prince of Wales. The British prince had sat there indifferently while the Kandyan artistes tried hard to please him.

'1922! Look, Ashley, it was in 1922 that my father came to Ceylon.'

'He must have made plenty of money,' said Ashley, patting Venugopalan's shoulder.

Venugopalan told Ashley the story he had heard: his father had had some property here. An estate and a couple of shops. What they said at home was that he had given all of it to a girl here. A girl in Kadugannawa.

'Was she your father's ... daughter?'

'Yes, there was a rumour like that as well. Her mother lived with Father for a long time, anyway.'

'Right! We'll find out. Like Mogallanan, we'll stand in the front yard and challenge them, I am entitled to a share of the property! Hey, it is the night of the new moon!'

With great enthusiasm, he took out a can of beer from his shoulder bag and opened it.

'March to Kadugannawa! Get ready, Mr Mogallanan!' Venu could not share his laughter. He wondered why he had told him that old story. He should have just seen the place ...

It was Ashley who was eager to see the botanical gardens and the orchids.

They left the town and took the mountain road. They went through two ghat sections and reached the top. Ashley asked the chauffeur to stop.

'Do you know the meaning of the word, "Kadugannawa"? A wayside rest-house.' The tiled roofs of the houses on the border of Kandy were visible from there and so was a curve of the Mahabali river which skirted Kandy.

They stopped in the middle of a small bazaar and Ashley said, 'This is Kadugannawa.'

He got down slowly from the car. A small bazaar with not more than thirty shops. Only two buildings were of concrete. The rest had tiled roofs.

'This is it?'

'Yes.'

There were tea estates on the distant slopes. Beyond them was the forest.

'Your father's name?'

'K.M. Nair.'

Three taxis were parked under a banyan tree. Ashley spoke to the drivers, then walked towards the shops.

Venu was astonished. Was this the town where Father had made a great name? Padinhare Angadi, the bazaar at home, was bigger than this.

Father was supposed to have owned two shops. Above both of them, on the first floor, were lodgings for the workers who had been brought from his village. Venu looked around uneasily. There were only two buildings with two storeys. There were small wooden railings under the blackened tiles.

Ashley came back after quite a while. He had with him an old man wearing a collarless shirt and a checked lungi. He had a big moustache and gentle eyes.

'This man knew my father-in-law. Ask him whatever you want. I'll interpret for you.'

'Ask him about the Malayalees who used to live here. Whether any of them are still...'

Ashley talked to the man at length. Then he said:

'Venu, he says there are no Kochiyans here now. They call you people Kochiyans.'

'Not now. Long ago. About forty years ago ...?'

Ashley and the man talked some more.

'There used to be a merchant. Then there was a *kattadia*—a magic-man, who cured people of their diseases with magic potions and incantations.' The building he pointed to was single-storeyed, a tiled, three-roomed structure.

When Ashley set out to explore the place again with the moustached man, Venugopalan said, 'No, Mr Ashley, let's go back.'

'But all these magic-men were your people.'

Perhaps ...

One of Amma's brothers had worked with Father for a while. They had fallen out with each other and parted company. Venugopalan had heard that he had worked with a Shingalathi widow, looking after her affairs. And that he had practiced magic for a while. He had never gone back to Kerala.

Ashley brought someone else. A young man in jeans with a cigarette dangling from his lips. Dragging his slippers on the ground, he followed Ashley, nodding agreement to everything he said. Venu felt there was a tinge of mockery in his smile. Ashley told him to get into the front seat of the car. He threw away the stub of his cigarette and lit another one. He offered one to the driver, who refused it.

'Where are we going now?' asked Venu impatiently.

'Would Mogallanan have gone back without making full enquiries? Mr Venu, are you sure this is the name of the place?'

Venugopalan grasped at this route of escape: 'No, I'm uncertain about it now. Let's go back, Ashley.'

'Let's have a look at the place he's talking about. It's quite nearby. He says there are some people there connected to a Kochiyan.'

They stopped the car in five minutes. Ashley and the young man got down and Venu followed reluctantly. As they turned into the lane, he saw white banners with something written on them tied to the coconut palms. Ashley explained that they were tributes offered to a dead person by relatives and friends and that it was the custom to put them up in the vicinity of the dead person's house.

Venu thought of a story he had once read in which a person goes in search of someone and finds ... a dead body.

'Are we ... are we going to a house where a death has taken place?' asked Venu in consternation.

'No. It's the third house from that one.'

There were a number of bicycles and scooters parked near the house where the death had occurred and people stood in groups on the roadside. One of them, who knew the young man, asked him something. The house they entered was very small. The space between the lane and the door of the house was full of shrubs. There was a pond by the side of the house and a man sat by the edge, gathering up the scum with a long pole. He wore a knee-length lungi and his face was not visible. The bones on his brown-skinned body stood out.

Ashley and the young man went up to him. Venu waited on the first step leading to the house. They kept asking the man questions, but he did not turn round or answer. His entire attention was concentrated on scooping up the scum. It looked as if he was not even aware of the two people standing next to him.

Ashley raised his voice and it sounded as if he was on the verge of a heated exchange of words. The man shifted the pole from his right hand to the left and slowly turned towards the visitors. The stubble on his face had patches of grey. Venu thought he saw anger blazing in his eyes. He spat at them and the spittle almost touched their feet. Then he looked up and said something loudly.

After that he turned back and continued to gather up the scum with the tip of his pole.

Ashley waited a few minutes, then walked back. The young man offered the man a cigarette, but when he went on with his work, unmoving, he joined Ashley, smiling.

Ashley said, 'Poor fellow, he's mad!'

As they walked back to the car, the young man kept talking. When they came up to the road, Ashley shook the young man's hand and thanked him.

When the two of them were alone in the car, Venu wanted to ask Ashley two things. One was the old man's name. But it was the second question he asked first.

'What was he doing? Wasn't it scum that he was collecting?'

'Yes, it was. Some people boil the scum and eat it. People who are very poor.'

Venu decided not to ask him the man's name.

After a while, Ashley said: 'It appears this man's mother was a Kochiyan's daughter. The people in the bazaar said she died a long time ago. The Kochiyan had a small shop. No one remembers his name.'

Venu tried to console himself. This could not be the town

where Father used to run a business connected with tea estates. It could not have been here that he made a great name.

'I asked him his mother's name, his father's name, his maternal grandfather's name, but he wouldn't say a word. When I shouted at him, he finally said something. A classic statement.'

'Yes ...?'

'That all Kochiyans are thieves!' Ashley laughed.

Venu made a feeble attempt to laugh with him.

'The woman who was supposed to be your father's daughter ... what was her name?'

Venu hesitated, then said, without meeting his eyes: 'I don't know.'

'What a shame! My father-in-law has some other friends in this area. It would have been easy to find out if you knew her name. This is the place, isn't it?'

'I don't know, Ashley. Perhaps ... perhaps I got the name wrong. It could be some other name like Kadugannawa ... Some of your place names ...'

'The next place we should visit is Sardiyel where there is a memorial to policemen who were slaughtered by a notorious gangster. Or Medovelayil, where there's a harvest festival. Or else ...'

'No, that's enough. I'm tired. Let's go back to Colombo.'

'Calambo, not Colombo. Let's go then.'

Ashley looked out. 'It gets dark early on the hills. And then it's new moon today.'

Ashley burst out laughing for no reason at all.

Venu felt that the voice describing the scenes by the side of the road came from very faraway. He lay back on the seat pretending to listen to everything, pretending to look at everything. While he kept repeating to himself:

'Yes, I mistook the name. The name of the place. I'm sure ... it's not Kadugannawa. It's some other name ... some other ...'

The Deluge

It was good that the door had been kept open. It was a Sunday, so it would be convenient for people to come. They could sit down wherever there was space. Vivek Joshi said that though the rain had stopped, the roads were still water-logged. Uncle Joshi and his family used to creep along in their thirty-year-old car at a snail's pace even in normal times.

Another group had arrived. Ramesh's family from Andheri. Ramesh had come early and gone out .to supervise some arrangements.

Bhaskarettan was sitting on the sofa, his eyes half closed, running his fingers over his forehead. Some of the visitors placed their hands on his shoulder and murmured words of sympathy. When it grew crowded inside, some people came out. It was on occasions like these that the small front yard between the house and the outer wall proved useful.

More people would come. Bhaskarettan had lived in the city for forty years and had many friends and acquaintances.

The unseasonal rains and floods were a constant topic of conversation among the vistors. Someone described how he had been trapped in his car on Friday evening in Dadar. Hundreds of cars had been caught in the rising waters, unable to move forward or go back.

'Finally, do you know what I did? I didn't look in front of

me or behind, I just opened the door and pissed! What else could I do?'

Only two or three people sniggered, listening to Bhonsle Sahib's feat.

'Have the children been informed?' A newcomer repeated the question many others before him had asked.

'I don't think it's possible to wait until they come. It's difficult for them to come at such short notice anyway. I spoke to them.' Ten years ago, there had been heavy rains in the city for three days continuously. The newspapers had estimated it as the heaviest rainfall in a hundred years. No one had estimated how heavy it was this time although many parts of the city were completely under water.

It had started raining on Thursday night. I had woken up to the sound of incessant rain. I had fallen into the habit of waking up at about two in the morning. I would drink a glass of water, go to the toilet and lie down again. I would wake up again only when the milkman rang the bell at five thirty. Just as I thought to myself that the rain that had started at night had not stopped. I noticed that water was splashing in through the tear in the wire netting fixed on the window to keep out mosquitoes.

Bhaskarettan groaned in his sleep.

'Such heavy rain! The water's splashing in.' I wondered whether Bhaskarettan had heard me.

I drew aside the plastic curtain and made an attempt to stop the rain splashing in by pressing on the torn wire netting.

'Come in, come in. Find yourself a place to sit.'

Ramesh, a friend of the family, had assumed the duties of a host. Now that he was there, Kadiri Sahib and Uncle Joshi went out. Playing host was not easy, especially on such occasions. Topics of conversation were hard to find. The floods in the city came in handy. The Malabari teashop owner who served tea free to people stranded in their cars in Dadar became a good subject for conversation.

'Move up a bit. You can sit here.'

There had been a bigger crowd here eleven years ago.

Remember? It was Ramesh who took over the arrangements that time as well. Our twenty-fifth wedding anniversary. The children insisted that we celebrate our silver wedding. The food was served in the hall of the colony club. A shamiana was put up outside for cocktails. Food was ordered for a hundred guests. The children calculated later that a hundred and forty people had come.

'Look, I bought the mobile phone reluctantly. That salesman bullied me into buying it. I really discovered how useful it is during these floods. Many people stranded on the way made good use of it.' That was Gangaram, who had set up a construction company after he retired.

When I got up on Friday morning I realised that the rain had not stopped. I did not think then that the incessant rain would become a flood.

There were no morning papers, no packets of milk in the plastic bags hanging on the front door. Water had stagnated in the yard outside the small verandah. A foul odour hung in the air, probably because the gutters were overflowing.

When I closed the door and turned, Bhaskarettan had turned on the light above the wash basin and begun to shave.

'So early ...?'

'I have to go out.'

'In this rain? Where?'

Bhaskarettan usually woke up to the whistle of the milk cooker. He would have three cups of tea one after the other, read three newspapers in full, make phone calls. At nine, he would go into the bathroom. He was very methodical about everything. In the old days, this routine used to change only if he had to take a morning flight.

He had taken charge of the advertisement division of a small newspaper four years ago. He had been the manager of a large advertising agency and had stayed idle for two years after he left it. He had had a large office staff, a car and driver at his disposal. Two or three dinners a week. For Deepavali, the house would be filled with gift parcels and there would be a sizeable bonus as well.

'Do you want to join this small newspaper?' I had expressed a doubt.

'I said I would help them for a short time. I'll try it for a year.' One year had become four. I had never asked what they would pay him. We never used to talk about his income. At the time we got married, he used to tell me everything without being asked. 'This is all I'll get in hand. We'll have to live within those limits.'

'It doesn't matter. I get about three hundred after all.'

'No—'

'What …?'

'You mustn't go to work anymore. We should be able to manage.'

I did not argue. I did not find it difficult to manage in the one-room flat.

It was Shanta Bhat and Chandrika Patel who told me about this colony, an hour's journey from the city. Their husbands had already booked flats there. I told him about it with some trepidation. He did not say anything.

'Think about it if it's feasible. We have two growing children.'

When the family property in the village had been divided, my elder sister had made me sign some papers and given me ten thousand rupees. The thought that it was in the bank gave me courage.

As the years passed, conversation at home had dwindled to bare essentials. But when we went to other people's houses for dinner, Bhaskarettan talked a great deal. He would crack jokes and make fun of me before his friends, calling me "the home department" or "boss". A mockery I enjoyed since it was loaded with affection.

The house had brought luck. I firmly believed that the change in his job and the rise in social status had happened after we came here. I prided myself secretly that it was the sale of the property in Vellinezhi and the ten thousand rupees I received for it that was the start of all this. Although I did not tell anyone that.

After the children were married, the house became very silent. They came once in two years and never stayed more than a week. They would pack a month's activity into that one week.

There were more people for the silver wedding than for the children's weddings. The congratulatory speeches made on the occasion were really worth hearing. The power behind Bhaskarettan's rise in his profession ... a symbol of silent service. What were the words? Once they had emptied three or four glasses and had a mike in their hands, the words tumbled out of their mouths. All the same, there was sincerity and goodwill behind all of it.

Bhaskarettan was always moderate, even at cocktail parties. Only I knew that the first glass he picked up would last him until the end. But he never failed to observe the rules, the courtesies. He would be full of laughter and witticisms. He had started life working in London for a year and a half. His friends used to say that he had acquired his pleasing manners there.

Bhaskarettan used to talk a lot the year before we got married. He would call up my office at the appointed time, to make sure when I would leave. He would arrive at the bus stop in front of Bierce and Company at least five minutes ahead of time. What a pleasure it had been to listen to the ceaseless chatter of this man who had become so miserly with words now. How often we used to burst out laughing during the two hours we spent together before we parted company at dusk at the gate of the hostel.

The children wanted to celebrate my sixtieth birthday. I evaded their requests. Bhaskarettan had neither agreed or disagreed with the idea.

The milkman had not come, so I quickly made some black tea.

'Where are you off to?'

He had come out in jeans, contrary to his usual practice.

'Jeans ...?' I smiled.

He did not seem to like my question.

'Why, are they prohibited?'

'No, no. Where are you going?'

'To Pune.'

'I wish you'd told me yesterday. Saroja's always been asking me to go to Pune.'

Saroja and Nambiar had been our neighbours when we stayed in the one-room flat in Matunga.

'I'm going on office work.'

I had seen the jeans in his suitcase six months ago when he returned from a business trip to Ahmedabad. I had watched him put it away carefully in the wardrobe and laughed to myself.

'I met the son of an old friend, a computer engineer. He insisted on buying it for me.'

'Which friend? Are there any of our old friends there?'

He had not replied to that.

Outside, the rain had not abated at all.

'What a downpour!'

'A car will come for me.' Bhaskarettan came to the door and looked out.

'Will you have breakfast? I can make some toast quickly.'

'There are three or four of us from the office. We've arranged to have breakfast at Lonavala.'

As the driver of the private taxi tried to decipher the door number in the rain, Bhaskarettan waved to him. He started to walk towards the car and I said,

'Wait. I'll bring an umbrella.'

He did not wait. He was quite wet by the time he got into the car.

The car had left by the time I could ask him when he would be back.

The milkman, his hair dripping wet in spite of the plastic sheet covering his head, got off his bicycle.

'The rain is terrible. There are all the signs of a real flood.'

The servant woman who swept the floor and cleaned the vessels had not yet come. It did not seem likely that she would come in this heavy rain.

There was water beneath the cot in the bedroom. I went to the bathroom when I was sure the rain had abated slightly. After my bath, I changed the wick in the small bronze lamp in front of the picture of Guruvayoorappan kept on a shelf hanging on the wall, lighted it and made an obeisance. As usual, I said my prayers in my mind. I had bought the picture and the lamp when we began to live in the flat in Matunga. I had intended to make the small room a puja room, but when Vasanthi had insisted that she have a room of her own, I had moved the picture, the lamp and the bowl of holy ash to a shelf on the wall.

When I went to the drawing room, I saw through the window that the rain had increased in intensity.

Normally, I would have made some semolina *uppuma* and ground some chutney to go with it. But I did not feel up to it. I ate three slices of bread.

When there had first been a hint of diabetes, I had reduced my intake of food. On Mondays, I ate nothing in the daytime. There was a saying in our villages that fasting on Mondays was good for a long married life. Luckily, Bhaskarettan had no ailments to speak of. Doctor Nadkarni said that regular food habits and half a tablet a day were all he needed. Bhaskarettan came with me to the doctor's once. The doctor suggested examining him and checking his blood pressure.

'I've no ailments of any kind, Doctor,' he said. Still, why don't you have yourself examined, I muttered in Malayalam.

'Why should I?'

Suddenly, he had looked angry. It's precisely because you lose your temper like this over small things that I felt the doctor should examine you, I said to myself.

For some time, I had used the face cream the children had brought before going to bed. Later, I stopped. When my hair started to grow grey, I used to go to the beauty parlour once a month and have it dyed. Then I thought, what use was it? The bill came to a hundred and twenty-five and there was the auto-rickshaw fare as well. At fifty or fifty-five, one turned grey anyway. How long could it be dyed black? After two of my teeth were removed, my cheeks had grown hollow. They would never be full again. Whether you were a man or a woman, you had to accept your age sometime. Wasn't I good-looking when I was young? That was enough. Now I was married and had two children. And they had three children of their own. That was good enough. I felt like telling Ramesh's wife all this whenever I saw her coarse, artificially blackened hair.

Bhaskarettan was a shade darker than me. And an inch taller. Nevertheless, his face looked young. Even now, women liked to hover around him at dinners and receptions. He was full of witticisms and old sayings twisted neatly to suit each occasion. Actually, even at this age, his face would be suffused with radiance when he laughed.

Someone once told me in the strictest confidence that Bhaskarettan had had a love affair before he got married. Not someone—it was the late Sharmaji's wife. I was already aware of this. He had stayed in her house as a paying guest when he returned from England. He had told me all about it. Her father was a Malayalee and her mother a Marathi. The girl had begun to take undue liberties with him. When he realised that her parents were encouraging her, he moved out. 'It was not a serious affair,' Mrs Sharma.

In a manner of speaking, you could say such things about me as well. Some evenings, I've walked with Satish Kumar, who works in the Radio Station. I've gone with him to the cinema and to coffee places. We've held hands as we walked. But I swear nothing else happened. Then there was Bhagavandas, personal assistant to the General Manager of my company. It was fun at that age to have many people say pleasant things and hover around me. It would be a lie not to admit that. I had gone to the record room to pick up a file. This Bhagavandas came up suddenly from behind and put his arms around me. I turned my face away, so his lips touched a spot below my ear. I felt the earth reeling around me. I was frightened. I stopped going to the record room alone. If I saw the fellow coming towards me while I waited for a bus, I would quickly withdraw into the crowd. When I saw Bhagavandas last year, I could hardly recognise him. He had become a grandfather many times over. I found it hard not to laugh when I recalled how crazy he had been over me once.

No one takes the minor involvements of youth seriously.

A woman once told me in great confidence: 'Rugmini, this is only for your ears. Bhaskarettan had a serious affair once.'

'Really?'

'It's the truth. He had a child by her. It was after that that he married you. It was a son. He looks exactly like Bhaskaran. Ditto.'

I wanted to tell that Sindhi woman that back in our village they would have described the child as the living image of the father.

My friends pitied me quite a bit when I got married. Rugmini was tall, fair-skinned, beautiful—she could have got someone with a better personality. She was carried away by the fact that he had worked in England.

Who knew what sort of a job he had had there?

To start with, Indians found jobs as porters and sweepers in England.

I had gone up to them quickly, to prevent them passing any more comments. All this gossip was being exchanged at the telephone operator, Girija's wedding.

I knew that it was because they had never heard him talk that they thought of Bhaskarettan's shortness of stature and dark complexion as problems.

Do you know, he wears trousers and a full-sleeved shirt even when he's alone at home? He changes into pyjamas only when he sits down to dinner.

When we started our life together, I used to ask him jokingly, 'Why are you all dressed-up? We're not expecting anyone.' Bhaskarettan would smile. 'In the African jungle, the white man shaves, polishes his shoes, changes for dinner. When he was asked the same question, the white man said: "I do this for my own satisfaction." You haven't seen that film of Chaplin where, starving and hungry, he boils and eats his shoes for Christmas, wearing a three-piece suit and using a knife and fork. Chaplin films are shown in the mornings. Watch them.'

Once, after attending a wedding, I said to him: 'The girl is no match for him at all. I wonder what he saw in her.'

We were on his scooter. Bhaskarettan said: 'Look, that whole area is a slum. You must look at it at night from a plane as it lands. It's beautiful! The glow of a thousand bulbs. It's the same place. Beauty and ugliness depend upon the person who sees, the point from where he looks ...'

He spoke in English. His pronunciation of English was different, wonderful. You could never tire of listening.

Wasn't it the Friday after the heavy rains started that I was talking about? The second day of the unseasonal rains. I used to telephone Ammini and Sarojiniedathi around noon. After that I would call Bhaskarettan at the office.

If I did not call Ammini, she would call me, just before she took a nap. I put a handful of rice in the cooker and warmed up the previous day's curry. It continued to rain outside. A soundless rain, without a wind, that filled me with a terrible dread. I thought it would never end. I had only heard of the flood that would occur at Kalpantham, when the world would end.

I dialed Ammini's number but could not get through. Ammini sometimes made kalan, a vegetable preparation with curd, and sends it across. Bhaskarettan was very fond of it. I had tried making it according to the recipe Ammini gave me but it did not turn out right. It was difficult to satisfy the tastes of a person who said he was thinking of writing a book on Kerala cookery.

I could not get Ammini's number. I tried Sarojiniedathi's. Sarojiniedathi had continued to stay in Bombay after her husband died. By herself. She was seventy now. Once a year, she organised the women's group dance, the Kaikottikkali, for the Onam festival. I used to take part in it until about six years ago. The rehearsals used to start four or five months in advance. Critical comments about the performance continued for three months after it was over. It seemed as if Sarojiniedathi stayed alone in the city only to arrange kaikottikkali once a year.

I could not get her number either. I tried Bhaskarettan's direct line at the office. The telephone had gone out of order because of the heavy rain.

Suddenly, the phone made a faint, whining sound.

'Hullo, is it Mrs Bhasker?'

'Yes, yes.'

'Oh, you don't know me. But I know you. I'm Mrs Gadgil, Shefali's mother. Shefali ... Bhaskar Saab's secretary.'

'Yes, I know her, though I didn't know her name was Shefali. I know of her as Miss Gadgil. She had called here a couple of times. I think I saw her once, in the office car. What is it, Mrs Gadgil?'

'We haven't met but I know all about you from Bhaskar Saab. How is your health now?'

'I'm all right.'

'Dolly's gone with Bhaskar Saab. We call her Dolly at home. Did he go by train or by car?'

'I don't know.'

He would get angry if I asked questions like that. Would he go to Pune by taxi or get off at the station? I didn't know.

'The rain is terrible. In the fifty-three years of my life, I've never seen such rains in Bombay. The radio said that there have been three landslides on the road to Pune.'

'Is that so? I don't listen to the radio.'

'They'll have trouble if they go by car. I was in the bathroom when she left. If you can ring up the office ...'

'Mrs Gadgil, I can't get outside numbers on my telephone. The only call I've had so far is this one from you. If you could call, Mrs Gadgil and let me know ...'

'I'm Mrinal. Call me that, Rugminiji. We know all about you. About your daughter in Dubai, your daughter in America, their children ... Saab has told us everything.'

'I'm glad, Mrinal. Mrinal must be short for Mrinalini, no?'

She laughed, sounding happy. When she put the phone down, I wondered whether I had the same kind of pain in my chest as I had once had when I had an attack of breathlessness.

Bhaskarettan had never told me that he had visited his secretary's house.

How old would Shefali be? The mother was fifty-three. She had mentioned her age, being a decent sort. The daughter could be twenty or thirty then, or somewhere in between.

I served out some rice and curry and placed the plate on the table. The phone rang. Maybe Mrinalini had some news. What a relief, it was Ammini.

'Ammini, why didn't you call? I can't get through to anyone.'

I felt I was on the verge of tears.

'I've been dialing your number for quite a while.'

It was raining as heavily there. Her husband had not gone out. The ground floor of his office was a godown and it was flooded.

'Ammini, don't hang up. I can't make outgoing calls. Bhaskarettan has gone to Pune. I don't know whether he's gone by car or by train.'

'Rugmini, how could anyone go out in this rain? Is he touched in the head?'

'If it was an official matter that had been fixed earlier, even an earthquake would not have deterred him. Don't you know how he is, Ammini? Someone called just now to say that there have been landslides.'

'Then they'll come back, what else? Don't worry so much.'

'Just call Bhaskarettan's office. Find out how they went to Pune, where they're staying and all that. Tell them I can't get through from here. And then call me, Ammini. You'll call back for sure, won't you?'

Ammini was my only connection with the outside world.

I felt relieved after I spoke to her. I ate a handful of rice. Suddenly, darkness filled the house. A wind which had been lying quiet somewhere came to life and joined the fury of the rain. When I saw the neem trees outside bend and sway, I realised how strong the wind was. I closed and bolted all the windows which were open. Although it was afternoon, it was pitch dark inside. I turned on the domed light in the centre of the room. The phone rang. I picked it up thinking it was Ammini. It was Mrinal Gadgil.

'Look, Mrs Mrinal Gadgil, didn't I tell you I can't make any calls from here? Call up the office and find out where they've booked rooms.'

'But Rugminiji, how will they reach Pune? They say nearly a thousand vehicles are stranded at Khandala. I called the office. They don't have any information. Bhaskar Saab is not a type who talks to everyone in the office. But don't be upset, Rugminiji. Bhaskar Saab is so mature, such a man of the world, so why worry?'

That was true. He was a type who would not lose his self-confidence even if he were surrounded by danger on all sides.

'If there's been a landslide, he'll find another route.'

I continued to listen to her. Let Mrinal Gadgil talk away, I thought. It was a comfort to listen to someone's voice.

'Hadn't the company decided to send Shefali out because she couldn't handle computers? It was Bhaskar Saab who insisted that she be confirmed.'

'Yes, he's a very kind-hearted person.'

'Her father and I separated when she was two. Bhaskar Saab is like a god to her.'

'Oh!'

'He's very fond of her too. When he went to Ahmedabad, she was the only one he took from the office.'

To Ahmedabad? He said the Circulation Manager and the Finance Manager were going with him. He had not mentioned the secretary at all.

'Didn't you like the jeans she bought him as a gift, Rugminiji?'

'Eh—what?'

'The jeans—'

'Oh!' I laughed heartily. 'I liked them very much. It must be because Shefali insists on it that he wears jeans at his age.'

'Isn't it the youthfulness of our minds that determines age, Rugminiji? I thought you would come for Shefali's birthday ...'

'I ...' What explanation could I give?

'Saab said you had a sudden dizziness and nausea. Saab was the only guest apart from a few relatives. It's the watch Saab gave her that day that she wears regularly now. You get whatever foreign articles you want here now, don't you?'

'Oh yes, in plenty.'

'Anyway, Rugminiji, what problem do you have to get them? With both your daughters living abroad ... It's difficult if you can't make a telephone call. I'll call again. I'm not worried at all since it's Bhaskar Saab ...' She laughed aloud and went on talking. Then she put the phone down.

For years now, I had had to remind him about my birthday very tactfully. When the children were with us, they used to each give me a card and say, "Many happy returns." Although Bhaskarettan was keen on observing the customs and formalities of the white men, he never bothered about remembering birthdays and wedding anniversaries.

Was the violent wind outside circling inside my mind as well? I prayed silently. I rebuked myself. It must have upset Bhaskarettan when both the girls got married and went abroad. It was not astonishing that her humility had awoken his affection. I scolded myself: why had I not realised he was a sixty-seven year old man who needed sympathy?

Mrinal's words, that I had not listened to properly, claimed my attention.

'He may be old in years, but he's young at heart, isn't he, Rugminiji?'

What had I said in reply? Had I grunted assent? Or laughed it off? I remembered the days when we were both young in body and heart. Years ago. A time when he had made onslaughts on my body night and day, to the point of exhaustion.

I walked up slowly to the closed window, opened it and peered out. The banana trees were bent double and almost touched the ground. The branch of a neem tree had snapped and hung down. The angry wind had not abated, nor the rain.

The phone did not ring again until dusk. When he went somewhere faraway, he used to call me as soon as he reached his destination. Later, he would call to say when he would start back.

If there had been a landslide at Khandala, he would have to come back. He used to go often to Pune when he was in the old company. I remembered that while his companions stayed in a hotel, Bhaskarettan always stayed in a guest house. Was it at the Agricultural College or the University? I recalled that he had told me he stayed there because they had large grounds where he could take a walk in the morning. He said the guest houses were more comfortable than big hotels.

The phone rang. To my relief, it was Ammini.

I asked her petulantly: 'How long you took, Ammini! Don't you know I can't make any calls?'

I held back my tears. We had at least a hundred close friends in this city. Couldn't they have called me from time to time? I was a prisoner in this small house, trapped between the storm and the flood.

'Look, Ammini, there's a place where he generally stays. A guest house. At the Agricultural College or the University. One of the two. Find out the number somehow. Sankarettan must have friends in Pune. Find out somehow if he's reached there. If you get him, ask him for all the news and call me. Won't you call me, Ammini? I am ...'

Ammini's voice changed. Was I making a nuisance of myself? She said she would try and put the phone down.

The darkness inside the house deepened. I turned on two more lamps. The rain continued to pour down with vengeful obstinacy. Mahalakshmi, the Goddess of Wealth and Prosperity, who presided over this city, must be disgusted, I thought. People had become so wicked. All one heard of every day was looting, murder, rape and kidnapping. Mahalakshmi must have allowed the city to be punished.

I had a wash, changed the wick of the lamp in front of the picture of Guruvayoorappan, poured in oil and lighted it. God, Bhagavan, may he come back safe.

He used to tell me in advance if he was not coming back at night. He would arrange for Krishna's daughter or Mrs Chatterji's houseboy to spend the night here. But he had gone to Ahmedabad saying he would return in three days and came back only on the fifth day. Krishna's daughter had come over and watched T.V. until midnight while I slept. There was nothing to fear even if I was alone. The houses were close to one another since it was a colony. There was a watchman at the gate. Still, it was a comfort to have someone inside the house.

I opened the front door slightly and looked out. When the wind swept in rain drops and dry leaves, I closed the door.

Mrinal Gadgil telephoned again.

'I've been trying your number for a long time but I couldn't get through. How are you, Rugminiji?'

'Oh, I'm all right.'

'If you have wheezing, it grows worse when it rains. I hope you are all right. You had angina earlier, didn't you? And now?'

'No, Mrinal, I'm fine.'

'You must have plenty of houses around since it's a colony. We live in an old flat, but there's a lot of space. The only problem is that we are on the fourth floor.'

It was a great comfort to hear a human voice from outside. But I wished she would not call again.

'Any news?'

'No, Dolly didn't call.'

I put the phone down. I turned on the T.V. The news was over. They were playing film songs. The girl who was singing was wiggling her hips and romancing with a young man. It was at least thirty years since I had gone to see a film. When a Malayalam film was shown here for journalists and they invited us, we went to see it. That was—let me see, in eighty or eighty-one. It was while I was expecting Vasanthi that we last bought tickets to see a film. Some film about an elephant. The elephant saves the hero. There is a fight in the jungle. The elephant dies, the hero looks at its carcass and sings a long song. I couldn't remember the name of the film.

It was wet, humid and cold. Even so, I felt thirsty. I drank three glasses of water. I wondered whether to make chapathies or warm up the leftover rice. I was not at all hungry.

I had no idea what time it was. The wall clock had stopped since the battery had not been changed. Where was my watch—in the cupboard or the drawer of the table? I used it only on rare occasions when I went out.

The phone rang, startling me. Bhaskarettan

It was Ammini.

'Look, Rugmini, Sankarettan called Pune. Guess what? It hasn't rained at all there!'

I remembered what my grandmother used to say. That at the end of the Kali Yuga, at the time of the Apocalypse, the Rain God would divide the country up and it would rain only in certain parts.

'And then?'

'Why didn't you tell me Vinitha is here?'

'But Vinitha is in Dubai.'

'Then who is it? Vasanthi? The Guest House Manager said that Bhaskar Saab has taken a room there and that his daughter was with him. It was I who spoke.'

I did not say anything.

'I didn't get Bhaskarettan. They were in the restaurant when I called. They asked me to call in half an hour. I'll call and then ...'

'Don't bother, Ammini. We know now that he's there. I'm relieved.'

I rang off.

I wandered aimlessly through the drawing room and bedrooms. I opened the windows. I thought there was a rhythmic cadence in the howling of the wind. I opened the front door and the water on the verandah swept into the drawing room. It spread over the carpet in the centre, changing the hue of the faded green.

The phone tinkled. When I lifted it, there was silence. The instrument was dead. No more outside calls would come to this house.

Standing at the front door, I was drenched. The chill tickled me. I could hear the rippling of the water that had collected in the front yard.

I stepped into the veranda. Darkness and the lapping of the water. The wind sounded as if someone was blowing through a hollow bamboo. Suddenly, the lights went out, even those at the gate and along the footpaths. I felt comfortable now that it was pitch dark. This was the deluge. When everything was submerged in the floods, didn't Bhagavan float over the water on a banyan leaf? What peace there must have been then.

I stretched out on the verandah, resting my head on the threshold. Cold fingers of water crept up from under my ribs to my back. Mischievous fingers that tried to turn me on my side, wet fingers that tried to tickle me. I imagined the city entirely engulfed in water and myself floating on the surface and laughed to myself. I was relieved, my mind was at rest, I was not afraid.

It was Sunday today. Those who were seated inside made room for the newcomers. Let everyone sit or stand in whatever space there is.

It's Shefali who has just come in. Yes, the figure I had seen in the office car is standing there unbuckling her sandals. Bhaskarettan sees her, sits up straight and looks at her. She sees a familiar face, walks towards her with relief and says something in a low voice. Bhaskarettan continues to look at her. So that, when she comes nearer to say something, he can open the floodgates of the tears he has been suppressing.

She looks around and says, 'I'll be back. I have to go to the airport, my uncle is coming at eleven.'

She goes up to Bhaskarettan before she leaves.

'I'm leaving.'

That's when something really funny happens. A wordless bit of fun. Only I can understand it. Bhaskarettan looks at her sorrowfully as if to say, you are all I have. She replies with a look. Shefali's eyes say, while the old woman was alive, it was great fun. But if you think I'm going to shoulder the burden of looking after an old man, forget about it! Then she walks out. Everyone there knows she won't come back. What can be funnier? I want to burst out into a raucous laugh. At least in order to wipe out the pleading look on Bhaskarettan's face. But I can't. They've moved the dining table and sofas to make space, covered my body and laid me out.

Had they brought in the dead body silently, with their heads lowered, murmuring something now and then, as we do in the villages in Kerala? When I came to North India, there were many local customs I could not reconcile myself to. But their funerals are good. They beat drums, shout "Ram Nam Sat Hai!" and treat the walk to the cremation ground as a celebration.

Let there be a celebration around my dead body. Ram Nam Sat Hai. Weren't most of the people who had come to the house North Indians? So the northern rituals and customs must be observed. Ram Nam Sat Hai!

Insight

It was a mistake to have assumed that the news would not have reached here.

She used to come by herself to her home in the village from time to time. No one used to be surprised by this.

She had a bath and breakfast and came and sat down in the verandah. Amma, her mother, went up to her and asked without any preliminaries: 'Sudha Kutty, is what we heard true?'

'What did you hear?' She gave her mother a harsh look, deliberating on how to build a wall of words around herself.

Amma closed her eyes and said softly: 'That you and Prabhakaran are separating ...' Amma had always had this habit of closing her eyes if she had something embarrassing to say. Sudha decided it was better to be aggressive than give her a direct answer.

'And who sends you news like this with telegraphic regularity?'

Amma sat down some distance away, stretching her legs out on the stone steps at the entrance. 'Sreedevi came to Narayanankutty's place the day before yesterday. Her Devu's husband is in Madras, isn't he?'

So her younger sister's mother-in-law was diffusing bits and pieces of news among the relatives.

'The news was in Visalam's letter yesterday as well.'

Once Chandri got the news from her elder sister, she would of course write to her mother.

Sudha stepped into the yard. It was only ten in the morning, but it was terribly hot. She kept close to the shade of the wall as she walked. As her pace quickened, her rubber slippers made a sound, tapping against her heels.

She often found excuses to come to this old house where her mother stayed by herself in search of solace. There was no telephone to disturb her. She did not have to dress up to entertain guests. She did not have to stay awake until Prabhakaran's executive friends left at midnight, listening to their jokes with a hostess's artificial smile clinging to her face. But then, she used to be given permission to come here only once in a while. And that, for three or four days.

The first question Amma asked was always: 'When do you have to go back?' This time, she had not asked. As she walked back to the verandah, Amma said, 'People keep saying all sorts of things. What really happened?'

She did not reply.

'As far as I could make out ...' Amma stopped.

'It's true, Amma. It's better for us to separate.'

Amma bent her head and stared at the steps.

The girl who helped in the kitchen came and asked her something and Amma got up and went in.

Sudha had taken leave for fifteen days from the bank. A few people at the bank had an inkling of what was happening. She had spoken frankly only to Nirmala Srinivasan, the Cashier. It was Nirmala who had arranged a room for her at the Y.W.C.A.

She had felt that Amma liked to live on her own. Amma did not encourage relatives or friends to visit her. If the children did not go and see her, she never complained. She wrote letters on inland letter-forms once a month to her three children, regardless of whether they replied or not. She always had a young girl from one of the neighbouring houses to help her. When Sudha came the previous year, Amma had told her that the girl who was then working with her was going to get married. She was going to give her a gold chain weighing a sovereign.

'All three of you must give her whatever you can. You can send a money order in Kuttiraman's name. Or in mine.'

Visalam and Chandri were to send three hundred rupees each and Sudha four hundred. Sudha was being asked to give more since both of them worked and they had no children.

When the girl left, her younger sister had come to help Amma in the kitchen.

Visalaedathi was anxious about Amma staying here alone. She had a large house in Thiruvananthapuram and many servants.

It was on an occasion when they had all gathered at home. 'If Amma falls ill, there's not even a doctor nearby,' Visalaedathi had said.

'I'm not going to fall ill,' was Amma's reply.

A black hen and her brood of chickens came hesitantly into the yard from the banana grove through a gap in the wall. They ran along the sides of the yard pecking at morsels.

Sudha heard Amma say: 'It's a wildfowl. It comes here every day at this hour. God knows where it comes from!'

Sudha looked at them, amused. The mother hen was frightened when she saw people in the house. Sudha moved towards them softly to take a closer look, keeping to the shadows. The mother hen clucked a warning and ran into the garden, followed by the chicks.

Amma did not say anything while they had lunch.

Sreedharettan, her younger sister's husband's elder brother, came in the evening. He was the Headmaster of the local High School and an important person in the village.

Sudha readied herself for a cross examination based on rumours he had heard. Pretending nothing had happened, she asked about his wife and children and complained about the absence of a breeze in summer.

'How many days leave do you have, Sudha Kutty?'

'A week.'

Amma interrupted. 'I don't have any milk, Sreedhara, to make you some tea.'

'I don't want any.'

Sudha was at a loss when small talk ran out. But Sreedharan began to talk about the oppressive heat in Madras, the wealth Jayalalitha had amassed, Karunanidhi's rule ... Sudha listened, contributing nothing of her own. When the conversation petered out, he got up to leave.

She had heard that this man's horoscope had also been considered at the time when marriage proposals were being discussed for her.

A swarm of dragonflies began to buzz around by evening. As a child, she had heard that dragonflies hovering low over the ground was a sign of rain. She wished it would rain. The heat in the month of Meenam here was no less that of the Vaikashi summer in Madras. Since they were still arguing about who would pay for them, there were no fans in the house.

'Sleep in the southern room at night. There'll be at least a faint breeze there,' said Amma as she served dinner.

'I can sleep anywhere.'

There was a rusty old table fan in Amma's room that Achan had bought years ago.

Sudha had not brought anything to read, nor had she picked up a book on the way. Achan's old books lay in a heap on the round table in Amma's room. Amma usually read for a while at night. There were no new books though. She glanced at the book that Amma had kept open on a copy of *A History of the World*. It was *Hima Giri Vihara* (Discourses from a Snow-capped Mountain).

A bed had been made in the southern room. She changed into a nightgown and looked at the time. Eight forty-five. In the city, Prabhakaran would be going back home after a game of rummy and two beers.

Amma walked in. 'You can bring that table fan in here if you want. It's a bit noisy, but it still works.'

'No, I don't need it.'

She sat down on the bed as if she was about to lie down, so that Amma would go away quickly.

'Still ...' Amma wanted to talk.

'Tell me.'

'Separating after having lived together for five years'
She did not say anything.
'What will people think when they come to know?'
She turned slightly so that she did not have to see Amma's face.

Relieved to have found a topic to speak about, she asked, 'How can you make a phone call from here if you need to?'

'There's a booth now in the room next to the pharmacy. You can call anywhere you want.'

She was drained of words again.

'What have you decided to do?'

'I'm thinking it over.'

'Do you want me to come and speak to Prabhakaran?'

Sudha said hastily, 'No, no.'

Amma gave her a pitying look. Trying to suppress her anger, Sudha said: 'There's no need to try to bring about a compromise, Amma.'

Amma went out.

Sudha knew Amma would not speak of this matter again. Silent acquiescence was part of her nature. Achan had died after a paralytic stroke had confined him to bed for a year and a half. Amma had never spoken to anyone of her suffering, of the cruel fate she had been subjected to. She had not heard Amma protest even when people had murmured to each other about how a stepsister had snatched away Achan's entire earnings.

Amma said to Sudha the next morning: 'Your Valiamma at Cholayil has sent word that she would like to see you.'

Sudha hesitated.

'The old woman heard the news from Janu, who brings milk here from the house next to Valiamma's.'

'I'll go and see her.'

'You said you'd go last time as well but you didn't.'

'All right, I'll go.'

'She's eighty-four. Who knows how long she'll last. She can't see a thing. But she's quite fit otherwise.'

Valiamma of Cholayil was Sudha's grandmother's older sister. Because Amma called her Valiamma, Sudha did too.

Valiamma used to come here to visit her younger sister. She used to like doing Visaledathi's hair in different ways. At dusk, she used to make the three children sit down and recite their evening prayers loudly.

Muthassi, her grandmother, would give Valiamma the bed and lie down on the floor. Valiamma liked telling the children stories. It was Sudha Kutty she always caught hold of. Visalaedathi would dodge her and Chandri would fall asleep. Sudha thought Muthassi too was half-asleep as she listened.

There was the story of how Unniyamma hid Palat Koman behind her long, flowing tresses while she bathed in a pond. Then there was the story of Kovalan and Kannagi. Later, when she visited Madurai, she had recalled this story that Valiamma had narrated. Valiamma had described how Kannagi had plucked out her breast, thrown it at the city and set the place on fire as if she had stood watching it happen.

She had wanted to buy a gift for Valiamma. But she had quarrelled with Prabhakaran about something just as she was about to go shopping and had lain down in the hotel room in protest until it was time for the train.

She had last seen Valiamma the day before her wedding, when she had gone to receive her blessing. That was more than five years ago. Even while her grandmother was alive, she had somehow been more fond of Valiamma. She had come home seven times in those five years. Yes, seven. Prabhakaran had been with her on two occasions. Valiamma used to ask for her every time. She lived hardly three furlongs away and yet, every time, she had not been able to visit her for one reason or other.

The wildfowl and her chicks came into the yard that day as well. They did not seem to be as frightened as they had been the previous day. She went a little closer. Yes, they were a mother and her chicks all right. She watched the specks of sunlight glint against their black, shining feathers and scatter on the ground.

'Here are some visitors ...' The chicks scurried away hearing the voice.

Sreedevi Amma and her younger sister stood in the yard. Observing courtesies, Amma was asking them to sit down, telling

Janu to make some tea. Giving Sudha an uneasy look, Amma went in. The look said: 'You'll hear a bellyful.'

'Sit down, Sudha. You mustn't take offence if I speak frankly.'

She did not sit down. She made an effort to smile and failed. 'Do speak.'

'Why beat about the bush? I have to speak out. If what I heard is true, things are pretty bad.'

Sudha managed a smile and said nonchalantly, 'It's bad, but there's no way out.'

Sreedevi Amma's face darkened. She looked meaningfully at her younger sister who took the hint and said, 'What Narayanan Kutty wrote is right. It will bring shame to the family.'

Sudha stood there silently.

'To live together for five years and then put an end to ...'

Sreedevi Amma looked at her sister as if hinting to her to go on.

'I'm sure there were faults and mistakes on his side, but you have to accept them. That's what marriage means. The things your mother endured!'

Sudha attempted to smile. What she had wanted to say at first was: 'The fault is mine, Sreedevi Amma, not Prabhakaran's.' But she decided not to say anything.

They kept talking. Even as a child, Sudha had mastered the astonishing capacity to shut her ears to conversations that she was not interested in. As she began to search for forgotten names, characters in novels, the topography of places she had seen when younger, the voices would suddenly grow distant.

Sreedevi Amma asked as they were leaving: 'Do you think everything I said was futile?'

She smiled. 'No.'

'Don't you think there's some truth in what I said?'

'Yes.'

She sighed in relief. 'What have you decided then?'

Sudha smiled and said: 'Let me think it over.'

Parting her lips in a wide grin to express her satisfaction at having succeeded in her mission, Sreedevi Amma left, followed by her younger sister.

Amma asked: 'When are you going to Cholayil to see Valiamma?'

'I'll go.'

Valiamma too must be getting ready to give her advice.

Sumathi, who had been with her in High School, came in the afternoon with her three-year-old daughter. She used to wait for Sudha every day near the area where the carpenters worked. The wart below her nose seemed to have grown bigger. She had been married before she finished her tenth standard.

Sudha pressed her to sit down but she would not.

'How are you Sumathi?'

'Oh, getting along.'

She wore a glittering saree of blue, violet and red. Her husband, who was working in the Gulf, must have brought it. He came home on leave for two months every two years. A heady fragrance enveloped Sumathi and gold ornaments covered her neck and arms.

'I heard you'd come. Will you be here for some time?'

'Yes, a few days.'

The following Monday, there would be a house-warming ceremony at Sumathi's new house. 'You must come for it, Sudha Kutty.'

'I'll come if I'm still here.'

The child was tracing flower patterns on her mother's saree with her fingers. Stroking the little one's hair, Sudha said, 'I've forgotten her name.'

'Karthika.'

Holding the child's hand, Sudha tried to draw her closer but the child whimpered and clung to her mother.

Sumathi came right up to Sudha and said confidentially: 'I heard there was something wrong ...'

'Oh, so you heard too ...'

'Shankarettan who comes to lay the mosaic tiles ... when his wife told me, I didn't believe her.'

Sudha grunted.

'Is it true, Sudha Kutty.'

She smiled. 'Yes, in a way.'

Sumathi's eyes widened in anxiety. Bending forward so that her forehead almost touched Sudha's, she said very softly: 'Don't assume that I'm advising someone who is more educated and knowledgeable than me. It's better in every way to be reconciled to living together.'

Sudha tapped her hand. 'Let me think it over.'

'It was a mistake to have decided not to have children now. Whether they were boys or girls, you would not have had these evil thoughts then.'

Sudha looked at Sumathi in surprise. And made a note in her mind of a good colloquial expression, "evil thoughts".

Sumathi left.

When Janu brought milk that evening, she said that Cholayil Valiamma had asked for Sudha again.

'You'd better go,' said Amma.

'I'll go tomorrow.'

'She's not in need of money. But give her something all the same. Visalam gave her fifty rupees when she went and the old lady told everyone she met about it for days on end.'

Amma laughed. This was the first time since she arrived that she had seen the gloom lift from Amma's face.

What if she said she was not going to compete with Visalaedathi?

She decided to leave on Monday. She would not wait for the two weeks to be over. There had been enough unpleasantness in the three days she had been here.

Should she call Hyderabad, she wondered. She had noted down the mobile number in the book in her handbag. And the direct number of his office in her mind.

There was no one to send to book her ticket. She would get into the ladies compartment. After all, it was only an overnight journey.

He had told her to call even from the village. 'If possible,' he had added.

The next day, after breakfast, she said, 'I'll go and see Valiamma.'

'Take Janu with you.'

'No, I don't need to.'

She first dropped in at the new house in the carpenters' work-area. Sumathi was so astonished and delighted, she did not know what to do. Two men were varnishing the windows under the supervision of the carpenter, Narayanan.

She walked around inside.

'Both bedrooms have attached bathrooms,' said Sumathi proudly.

Sudha found it difficult to evade the invitation to have something to drink.

'He's written to say he's coming in July.'

'Ask him to take you to Dubai. You can see the place too.'

'That won't happen. He said only people with high salaries can afford that.'

All the same, Sumathi was very happy.

'I must leave now, Sumathi. I want to drop in at Valiamma's place.'

'Remember what I told you?'

'Of course.'

She turned and smiled.

Once she had passed the cluster of bamboos, she saw the stream, now run dry. There used to be bramble thickets on both sides. Water used to flow plentifully through the stream all the year round. In the rainy season, it used to overflow into the channel below and form a minor tributary of the river.

The house had been built in Valiachan's, her great-grandfather's, time. There was a bamboo stile now in place of the gatehouse. Sudha went up the steps into the front yard. There was no one around. Pepper had been spread out to dry on a bamboo mat. As she stood there hesitantly, Thankedathi came into the verandah.

'Look who's here! Achamma was complaining this morning that you were going to leave without seeing her.'

Thankedathi insisted that she sit down on the chair that was placed next to the wooden ledge with a back-rest, and began to talk about her family. Both her sons were studying and had gone back the week before to the hostel because they had practical examinations. Her youngest, a girl, was in the ninth standard. When their mother died, her younger sisters had taken their share of the property, built houses in their husbands' village and settled down there.

'They palmed off this crumbling old house on me. There was no one to speak for me.'

Her voice trembled in customary tribute to her husband's death. She wiped her dry eyes.

'Where is Valiamma?'

'In the northern room. She can't see at all. And she doesn't like anyone leading her by the hand. Who knows when and where she's going to stumble and fall.'

Sudha heard Valiamma's voice at the door: 'No one's going to have trouble on my account.'

Valiamma placed both her hands on the door frame and put out her foot accurately onto the verandah. Sudha hurried up to her. At eighty four, Valiamma held herself erect, without the slightest trace of a stoop. Her blouse and upper cloth were pristine white. Starch glistened on her bordered mundu. The radiance Sudha remembered from childhood had not dimmed at all. Sudha looked particularly at the thickness of the knot of grey hair. Whenever she listened to the story of Unniyamma, she used to imagine that it was Valiamma herself who undid her hair and hid Komappan inside it.

Thankedathi was about to pull up a chair but Valiamma said: 'No, I'll sit here. Sit down, Sudha Kutty.'

Valiamma's hand stretched out more or less exactly towards her arm. She sat down next to Valiamma on the wooden ledge.

'You've put on weight, Sudha Kutty!'

Sudha looked at her own arms. It was true, she had put on weight.

'You were gasping when you took a few steps towards me. I can guess even without seeing you, from your breathing.'

Valiamma smiled. There was no life in her eyes, but her face was free of wrinkles. Age had furrowed only her neck.

'Thankam, make some tea. And if there's any jackfruit, fry some.'

Sudha said, 'No, I don't want anything. Just half a glass of tea.'

Valiamma was obviously waiting for Thankam to go into the kitchen.

'What have you decided, child?' Valiamma's question was very sudden. Sudha felt confused.

'Don't worry. I didn't send for you to scold you or find fault with you. It's four or five years, isn't it, since we met?'

Sudha felt relieved.

'All these creatures here grin when I speak of what I see. They wonder what a person both of whose eyes are clouded with cataract can see. Can they see as much as I can?'

She had raised a voice a bit, probably so that Thankedathi could hear her from the kitchen.

Valiamma lowered her voice again. 'What have you decided?'

Sudha suddenly felt disturbed. Her breathing quickened.

'If you feel you've had enough of him, you should put an end to it. Marriage is a personal matter. There's no point acting out a charade just to convince the people around you.'

Sudha sighed, drew up her legs and sat facing Valiamma. Valiamma moved her head closer.

'My first husband none of you would have seen him.'

'Amma's seen him. He was a music teacher, wasn't he, a *bhagavathar*?'

'That was the problem. His music classes were at the Pisharoty's place. And he ate in our house. He was a fine singer. Wore ear studs set with red stones and had a sandal paste *tilakam* on his forehead. You can take it that I too found him attractive.'

Valiamma ran her fingers through her hair and chuckled.

'He went away before a year was over.'

'Yes, Amma told me.'

'He didn't go because he wanted to. I told him to go,'

murmured Valiamma. She smiled, fixing her sightless eyes on a spot in the distance.

'He didn't have anything material to give me. I could have overlooked that. But he would act coy and speak with a lisp, like a woman. Shouldn't men be smart and lively? I told him to his face that it was better to end the relationship, there was no other way.'

Sudha had heard about Valiamma's first marriage, but had not known the details.

Then Grandfather, her Valiachan, had come along. He worked for the Salt Department. They had had three children. Valiachan had died and all the three children died too. Valiamma still survived.

'You've seen Valiachan, haven't you? He wasn't handsome or good-looking or anything like that, was he?'

'I've seen him when I was a child. He was ill and confined to bed.'

'There was no one like him in this whole area. He would be right in front for the festival procession. If the elephant ran amuck, they needed Madhavan Nair. Only he could deal with fireworks that burst into eighteen levels of colour!'

Thankedathi brought the tea. Valiamma maintained a serious expression while she stood there. As soon as Thankedathi turned to go in, Valiamma laughed.

'Those who looked at him from outside saw him as a fierce cobra. He would lose his temper, quarrel and scold. Only I knew how soft and gentle he was. I only had to say I had a cold and he would be concerned and anxious.'

Valiamma's laugh grew louder.

Sudha forgot the problems she had been trying to keep at bay. She heard what Valiamma was saying with the same pleasure she used to feel when listening to her narrate stories long ago.

'Having no worries at all can be upsetting. It was after I had Kuttyarayan ...'

'What?'

'An upheaval ... An obsession for a man. I told myself,

control yourself, wretch. But it was no use, you understand. Still …'

Valiamma opened her mouth wide and laughed, without completing the sentence. Sudha realised that she had lost only her grinders, all her other teeth were intact.

'I was just your age then.' Valiamma sighed.

'Is he still alive, Valiamma?'

Valiamma's face dimmed.

'He's gone. They're all gone. I'm the only one left. I have to wait until I'm called. One can't make oneself die …'

Valiamma shook her head as if she was trying to get rid of something, slid back and rested her head against the wall.

'The other person. Who is it, Sudha Kutty?'

Sudha was startled. 'What?'

'You saw a man. You liked him. You decided it was him you wanted to live with. Isn't this what happened?'

'Who told you?'

Valiamma drew up her knees. 'No one has to tell me these things. Who is it, child?'

She found it difficult not to show how embarrassed she was.

'Is it someone you work with?'

'No.'

She would not be able to explain it to Valiamma. She had met him at a dinner organised to say goodbye to Janardan Rao, the manager who had been transferred. Janardan Rao, who claimed to be a singer, was singing a ghazal. The chief guest, the organisers and the clients who had been invited were all drunk. He was standing by himself at the other end of the room with a glass of orange juice in his hand. He looked at her from time to time, then slowly made his way towards her. She said to herself, her mind full of fear, 'God, these footsteps are coming straight into my heart.'

She was happy when he told her that he spent ten days in Madras every month. He saw people coming towards them and said, 'I guess I can call you at the bank.'

She nodded. She could not ask him why he wanted to call.

Valiamma asked: 'Is he married?'

'No.'

'Does Prabhakaran know?'

She paused for a while before answering. 'He knows something.'

'Then you should separate. He'll find another woman. That's not a serious matter. You must separate.'

Sudha was amused.

'It's not as easy to separate as it used to be in the old days, Valiamma.'

'If you don't want each other, that's the end of it. Isn't it?'

The confidence to explain without feeling embarrassed came back to her.

'It's not like that. The couple have to file a joint petition. The Judge will summon them after six months and ask whether they still wish to separate. If they say they do, they have to wait another six months.

She saw anger spread slowly over Valiamma's face.

'If two people love each other and want to live together, does the Judge have to give his consent?'

'That's the law, Valiamma.'

Valiamma was not satisfied at all.

'True, if there are children, arrangements must be made to maintain them. But what has the Judge to do with people who want to live together?'

'That's the law.'

'Law indeed! Don't provoke me to speak my mind.'

Thankedathi came to fetch the empty glasses. Valiamma kept muttering soundlessly to herself. Thankedathi said: 'Until last year, Achamma could make us out as shadows. Now she doesn't see even that much.'

Sudha said: 'An operation will restore your vision. A lot of people do it even at your age. I can take you to Madras if you want.'

Valiamma's laugh was bitter.

'No, no. Why should I get back my vision? I've seen enough, my child!'

Sudha got up to go.

Thankedathi said: 'Have your lunch here.'

'Oh no. Amma would have cooked for me.'

'The rice is on the boil. You must drop in next time you come, Sudha Kutty.'

Thankedathi went in. A fourteen-year-old girl arrived at the bamboo stile and moved it. Valiamma's eyes went to the entrance. The girl removed her slippers just below the verandah, looked at Sudha, smiled and went in, her head bent, not making a sound. When she was at the door, Valiamma asked:

'Where have you been?'

The girl trembled. 'To the Pisharoty's place, to get a book from Sarada.'

'And do you have to get dolled up in a silk skirt to go there?'

The girl went pale and scurried in fearfully.

Valiamma turned towards Sudha. 'She didn't have a book in her hand, did she?'

'No, she didn't.'

'The moment I heard it rustle, I knew it was a silk skirt.'

'She's only a child after all, Valiamma.'

'She's too grown-up for her age. I can see ...'

'I'll go now.'

Valiamma stood up.

Sudha remembered what Amma had said and quietly opened the purse in her hand.

'No. You're going to give me some money. Don't. What need has Valiamma for money?'

Taken aback, Sudha shut her purse.

'When you come ... when you come next ...' Valiamma's voice broke. 'If I'm alive, you must come and see me. That's all I ask.'

She saw Valiamma's lustreless eyes fill with tears. Tears filled her eyes too, she could not hold them back. She bent down and touched Valiamma's feet, seeking her blessing. Remembering that she had done the same thing five years ago.

Valiamma placed her hands gently on Sudha's bent head.

'May it turn out well this time at least.'

She walked out. As soon as she reached the bazaar, she noticed the board of the S.T.D. booth in the distance.

She murmured both the telephone numbers to herself. She had to check the mobile number from her notebook before she called. If she hurried home after the call, she would not miss seeing the wildfowl and her chicks come into the yard.

She quickened her pace.

Glossary

Achamma	father's mother
Achan	father
Ammaman	uncle
Bhagavathar	music teacher
Bhagavathi	the goddess
Bhikshu	Buddhist monk
Bhikshuni	female Buddhist monk
Brahmarakshas	the spirit of a dead Brahmin who died a gruesome death
Chandu	a paste used to make a round mark on the forehead
Chechi	older sister
Cheruman	farmhand (also called pulaya in Malayalam)
Chovva	evil that occurs when the planet Mars falls on certain signs of the zodiac
Edathi	older sister
Ettan	older brother
Flood of '99	is the Malayalam Era 1099 which is equal to 1924
Illam	traditional Namboothiri household
Kadumanga	a pickle made with small mangoes
Kalan	a curry made with vegetables and curd
Kanji	rice gruel

Kanni	second month on the Malayalam calendar, approximately September to October
Kaikottikkali	a group dance by women
Kasturyadi	Ayurvedic tablet for easing breathing trouble
Koothu	a narrative usually performed only within temple premises (given by *Chakyar*, the narrator-performer)
Kothankallu	a game played with small pebbles or stones
Meenam	eighth month on the Malayalam calendar, approximately from mid March to mid April
Mundu	a cloth worn round the waist
Muthassi	grandmother
Nallukettu	a sunken courtyard in the centre of a house with wooden pillars at the corners
Oppa	older brother
Pativrata	chaste woman
Payasam	a sweet made with milk and rice
Pottu	spot; the round mark, usually, on a woman's forehead
Prasadam	sandalwood paste, flowers etc. received from temple; this is sometimes accompanied by fruits and other offerings as well
Sindooram	coloured powder used to make a mark on the forehead
Taravad	extended family; also used for the house in which the family lives
Tayambaka	a rhythmic display exclusively of drums; a very special temple art form
Thorthu mundu	longish towel, sometimes worn instead of a *mundu* by workmen
Thirovonam	the tenth day of the Chingam month, commemorating the return of Mahabali (Maveli of the legend)
Thulam	third month on the Malayalam calendar, approximately October to November
Thilakam	a mark made on the forehead

Vaidyar	practioner of indigenous medicine
Vaikashi	from May to June
Valiachan	father's older brother
Valiamma	mother's older sister
Velichappadu	a dancer in the Bhagavathi temple. He becomes possessed by the Goddess and functions as an oracle
Veshti	a cloth worn over the shoulder (the 'second' *mundu*)
Vibhuti	holy ash
Vrischikam	name of the fourth month on the Malayalam calendar, approximately November to December

Other Titles in the Series

PRATIBHA RAY: *The Primal Land*
Translated from the Oriya *Adibhumi* by Bikram K. Das.

Soma Muduli, the patriarch and Soma Sisa, the rebel, both lie dead on the mountain: but with the dawn comes hope of a new beginning, as the infant Soma is born. Can the tribe survive?

The Primal Land (translated from the Oriya original, *Adibhumi*) is the saga of the embattled Bonda tribe, which has roamed free among the mountains of Koraput (Orissa) since time began, but now faces extinction.

SUBHODH GHOSH: *Shock Therapy*
Translated from the Bengali.

Subodh Ghose's stories are marked by a strong, vigorous narrative style and a lively universe of people and places drawn from the writer's formidable range of life experiences.

This collection of translations into English presents a number of his better-known stories. Romantic lovers, desperate peasants, eccentrics, conmen and patriots, persons with strong convictions or strange obsessions: all act out their lives in settings rural and urban, making the reader a witness to several segments of reality in a vividly evoked world.

BANI BASU: *The Enemy Within*
Translated from the Bengali *Antarghat* by Jayanti Datta.

This translation from the Bangla *Antarghat* is the story of a group of young friends who had committed themselves idealistically and politically to the Naxalite movement that rocked Bengal in the 1960s. Many years later, they still carry the scars beneath their lives of surface calm. But they also share the secret of a betrayal, one that was fatally injurious to some. Into this fragile, obscure universe arrives their betrayer, ironically seeking anonymity. Jagged wounds reopen and death follows. Is it suicide or murder, expiation or vengeance?

MANJUL BHAGAT: *Anaro and Other Stories*
Translated from the Hindi by the author.

Translated from the Hindi by the author herself, here are stories of women, men and children—all wrestling with life, not from positions of strength, but nevertheless holding on to their dreams.

From the unforgettable, feisty portrait of Anaro who refuses to be cowed down even in the face of unending drudgery or Taiji who is condemned as 'kabaad' by her family, but finds solace in her affection for Mangto, the kabadiwallah, to the tender tale of friendship between Bebeji and the tandoorwala—they all bear the perceptiveness, compassion and ingenuity of a gifted storyteller.

RAJAM KRISHNAN: *When the Kurinji Blooms*
Translated from the Tamil *Kurinjithen* by Uma Narayanan and Prema Seetharam.

Translated from the Tamil *Kurinjithen*, Rajam Krishnan's lyrical, erudite novel is a family saga of three generations of Badagas in the Nilgiris. As the winds of social change and modernity invade their protected lives, the innocence and harmony is replaced by conflict and tragedy that precede a new beginning.

MANNU BHANDARI: *The Great Feast*
Translated from the Hindi *Mahabhoj* by Ruth Vanita

A bold exposé of the contemporary Indian political scene that has cast aside morality and ethics and unfailingly betrays public trust for vested interests and private ends.

The novel opens with the death of Bisesa—an unknown village youth—in itself an insignificant event. But with an important by-election around the corner, the feasting begins as opposing political parties like vultures seize upon the unfortunate event to extract political capital out of it, thereby providing sharp insights into the exercise of power and patronage.

ASHOKAMITRAN: *Sand and Other Stories*
Translated from the Tamil by N. Kalyan Raman and Gomati Narayanan.

Written with the deepest empathy for women trapped by an almost absolute lack of resources—financial, intellectual, emotional—these stories by Ashokamitran have all the identifiable characteristics of his writing—irony, interiority, sensitivity.

The narrative in all three novellas—*Sand, Malati, Those Two*—moves in a series of short scenes, building tension with a relentless layering of detail. The exploitation of the women (Sarojini, her mother, Malati, Vaala, Dharam) and their daily struggle against it lies exposed in all its terrifying ordinariness.

MALAYATOOR RAMAKRISHNAN: *Roots*
Translated from the Malayalam *Verukal* by V. Abdulla.

Increasingly possessed by a yearning to escape the ennui of an indifferent marriage and the empty but comfortable lifestyle of a bureaucrat, Raghu decides to visit the small patch of ancestral property in his native village.

As he relives the past, old grudges are aired exposing the faultlines in relationships but also subliminally forging bonds with the land and his people.

The novel moves between the two worlds—the past and present—with pungent, earthy humour and sharp insights. The narrator's voice as he recounts the sights of his land and his experiences is powerful, sensuous and direct and moves inexorably to the apocalyptic moment when he finds his roots.

NAZIR AHMAD: *Son of the Moment*
Translated from the Urdu *Ibn-ul-Waqt* by Mohammed Zakir.

In the charged atmosphere of the Mutiny (1857), an English officer and a Muslim gentleman are brought together under remarkable circumstances. The Englishman persuades Ibn-ul-Waqt to adopt an English lifestyle as a means of drawing his tradition-bound compatriots to a more 'progressive' way of life. The consequences that follow are not what they had envisioned.

ASHAPURNA DEBI: *The First Promise*
Translated from the Bengali *Pratham Pratisruti* by Indira Chowdhury.

Set in the late eighteenth and nineteenth centuries, this widely acclaimed novel commemorates the struggle and efforts of women, of the mute domestic space, starkly neglected by history. As it tells the story of one of the many unknown women from the ignored interiors of Bengal, it also captures the larger social and cultural transformations of the colonial era.

Indira Chowdhury's confident translation, with its conscious choice of Indian English equivalents carries across the language divide, the flavour of Ashapurna's unique, idiomatic style.

SHARANKUMAR LIMBALE: *Towards an Aesthetic of Dalit Literature: Histories, Controversies and Considerations*
Translated from the Marathi *Sahityache Saundaryashastra* by Alok Mukherjee.

The first critical work by an eminent Dalit writer to appear in English, it is a provocative and thoughtful account of the debates among Dalit writers on how Dalit literature should be read.

The book includes an extensive interview with the author, an exhaustive bibliography and a critical commentary by the translator, Alok Mukherjee.